WHAT OF TERRY CONNISTON?

BOOKS BY BRIAN GARFIELD

Fiction / The Lawbringers / Vultures in the Sun /
Seven Brave Men / The Vanquished / The Last Bridge /
Valley of the Shadow / The Hit / Sliphammer /
The Villiers Touch / Sweeny's Honor /
What of Terry Conniston? / *Nonfiction* /
The Thousand-Mile War: *World War II in Alaska & the Aleutians*

What of Terry

A FALCON'S HEAD SUSPENSE NOVEL

BRIAN GARFIELD

Conniston ？？？

THE WORLD PUBLISHING COMPANY

New York and Cleveland

Published by The World Publishing Company

Published simultaneously in Canada
by Nelson, Foster & Scott Ltd.

First printing—1971

Library of Congress catalog card number: 72-133480

Printed in the United States of America

WORLD PUBLISHING
TIMES MIRROR

WHAT OF TERRY CONNISTON?

CHAPTER **One**

Carl Oakley walked out of the sagging barn and blinked when the hard sunshine hit his face. He snugged the dark glasses against the bridge of his nose and stood, feet apart and arms akimbo, squinting up the sun-bright dusty street of this dead and gone town that had once been called Soledad.

His right shoe intersected a narrow tire track faintly traced in the gravelly dust. Too narrow for the big car, Oakley judged; it must have been Terry's rump-jolting little sports car that left this print. He squatted on his haunches, elbows on knees, and brooded upon the dim track. It pointed into the barn, or away from the barn; in any case the barn was empty.

Beyond doubt this was where they had held her. There in the barn they had concealed the cars.

He rose to his feet with easy coordination and looked up the length of the ghost street. Beyond the abandoned wreckage of the buildings, two hundred yards away at the head of the town, Diego Orozco's obese shape waddled slowly, head down, looking for sign. Carl Oakley shook his head. *You won't find anything more. They were a smart bunch—we won't find anything they didn't want us to find.*

Five of them—four men and a girl—had kidnaped Terry Conniston. They had brought her here.

Oakley made a slow full turn on the balls of his feet, sweeping the horizons, the weathered tumbledown shacks, the drought-bleached desert. He was a tall man with a swimming-pool tan and a neat head of hair peppered with gray. His shoulders and waist were just beginning to put on a layer of office fat. His face, photogenic as an actor's, looked young and frank—always an asset in the courtroom. He was forty-six.

He put a cigar in his mouth, unlit. The hollow dark maw of the old barn loomed, sinister with empty shadows. It had likely been one of the highest-priced snatch cases since the Lindbergh caper, he reflected, but even the police and the FBI weren't in on it. Oakley couldn't afford to let them find out. It would cost him twenty times what the kidnapers had got. Nobody knew about it—nobody but Orozco and the two back at Conniston's ranch.

The old general store still had its roof intact. He gave it narrowed scrutiny. Was that where they'd held her? Trussed her with ropes? Had they fed her? Ignored her? Done unspeakable things? Here, perhaps, where the earth was scuffed, they had battled among themselves, leaving one dead. A quarrel over the spoils? And the second one, dead but not by violence—murder, disease, accident?

Terry Conniston: where was she? What had they done to her (or she to them, knowing Terry)?

They had been amateurs. Carl Oakley was a good country lawyer with a healthy respect for professionalism: it graveled him that a crew of second-rate musicians could bring it off. The untidiness of it disturbed him.

Let them have the ransom; the money, after all, had been Earle Conniston's and Earle couldn't complain. But Oakley had to know whether Terry was alive. And if she was alive where was she? What had happened to the last three members of the gang?

Oakley's orderly mind recognized the probabilities. They had probably killed her, probably buried her somewhere out there in the desert. But Orozco's hired *chicanos* had combed the district. They had found the two bodies but Terry hadn't turned up.

The awful uncertainty hung over him like a blade, poised and motionless but ready to cut. If she was still alive she could make bad trouble. Very bad trouble.

His glance traveled past the town to Orozco, fat and dogged as an ox, keening the earth with eyes like microscopes. Oakley removed the cigar from his mouth, feeling the heat; he dragged the back of his hand across his lips. It was time to call Orozco off. There was nothing more to be found here.

He sang out, calling Orozco down, and walked slowly toward the car, shoes scuffing the dust. Orozco met him by the car. "I didn't find nothing yet."

"You won't. It's been too long—the trail's gone too cold."

"This here desert can preserve things a long time," Orozco said with his faint trace of accent. He was huge and disordered in Levi's and khaki shirt, the vast balloon of his belly making a precarious arc pendulant over his belt. He wore a black moustache, like a bandit, and a little round hat.

Orozco said, "We still got two–three hours of good daylight. You sure you want to go back?"

"We're not going to find anything," Oakley insisted, his voice climbing to an unreasonable pitch.

"Well, you don't know that till you finish looking."

Oakley had bitten the cigar cleanly in two. He spat out the wet end and jammed what was left into the corner of his mouth. "Where'd they go, Diego? What did they do to her?"

"I don' know, Carl. I honestly don' know." Orozco lifted his fat arm southward toward the hazy peaks. "Maybe Mexico yonder. That's where I'd go with all that money. No more than a fifteen-mile walk from where we're standing—easy enough to crawl through the fence."

"No. They wouldn't have taken Terry with them if they'd gone on foot. Besides, the money was damn heavy. And if they went on foot, what happened to the cars? They had two cars here. Crap."

"Why should they take Terry with them?"

"I don't know, but they didn't leave her here, now, did they?"

"Okay, okay. I got no answers yet, Carl. I wan' to have one more look in that barn."

"Suit yourself."

The fat man walked away. Oakley got into the Cadillac, started the engine and turned on the air-conditioning. He had parked in the shade but that had been morning; the sun had moved around. The car was an oven. *Next time I park inside the barn.* Next time: but what was there to come back for?

He removed his hat and picked up the manila file folder from the seat, opened it and flipped through to the photograph he wanted. He sat inspecting it with dry hot air from the dashboard blower roughing up his hair. Floyd Rymer looked out of the photograph, straight at the camera, with a hard challenge and a hint of a secret smile. The whole mystery always came right back to Floyd Rymer: Floyd lay curled at the bottom of Oakley's mind like a sleepy reptile waiting under a sun-baked rock.

He wished he knew a little more about Floyd's baffling character. Private detectives across the country—Orozco's correspondents—had spent the past eighteen hours and a good sum of Oakley's money prowling Floyd Rymer's history; all they had turned up were dry vital statistics and a few clouded hints. Floyd had been born in Cincinnati to a family of Depression-poor alcoholics and gone through thirty years with hardly a ripple to mark his backtrail—a singularly anonymous figure, considering the force of his arrogant personality. No one was likely to forget him; but there wasn't anything useful in what anyone remembered of him.

Oakley's file had been flown in last night by Lear Jet from Phoenix. It contained six onionskin pages, typewritten, and a dozen glossy publicity stills of Floyd's nightclub combo. For at least three years it had been billed as The Rymers—booked around the circuit of second-string clubs from El Paso to Seattle. The picture on his lap was a good likeness of Floyd according to the scribbled marginal remarks. Floyd slouched hip-shot against his electric organ with his hands in the hip pockets of tight trousers. It was a long spare figure, sinewy-masculine. Shaggy black hair, tousled and thick, running down into heavy sideburns; brutal hooded eyes, pale gray or blue, with a calm air of cold disdain: amoral, predatory, taut with flashing hunger. Floyd looked like a creature who couldn't be reasoned with, appealed to, even frightened: a chilled primitive being, logical but emotionless, untouchable by the things that would affect ordinary people—wholly unpredictable because, his likeness implied, none of the usual rules would apply. The photo recalled to Oakley's mind the young captured SS officers he had seen in France in 1944.

The file didn't give away much. He sorted photos, scrutinizing their faces one by one.

Georgie Rymer, Floyd's brother. Wire-thin, pouched eyes, gaunt features with a bovine expression. According to the notes Georgie was a hopeless heroin addict who'd been in and out of institutions. In the photo he stood hollow-chested over his string bass, used up, a mere bookmark to indicate the place where a man had once been.

Theodore Luke, the drummer, perched heavy on his throne behind a set of drums and cymbals: a thick muscular grotesque, his face averted in all the photos. It was a disfigured, wrecked face, the result of a childhood car crash and inept plastic surgery.

Mitchell Baird, guitar: a newcomer, shown only in the most recent of the stills. He stood, a bit awkward, off to one side of the bandstand, aware he was still an outsider. Mitch Baird was twenty-three, the youngest of them. Chunky, sandy-haired, nice-looking in a varsity way: an aimless college dropout from a decent family. Orozco's stringers had traced him easily. He had drifted into trouble, joining a folk-rock band in New Mexico, getting busted at an afterhours party for possession of marijuana. First offenses usually rated suspended sentences but Mitch Baird had been unlucky: he had drawn a stiff-necked superior court judge who'd imposed a six-month sentence on him. Evidently a junkie in prison had steered him to the Rymers and he had joined the band a month or two ago in Tucson.

The only picture of the fifth member of the gang was a blurred old snapshot from a small-town junior high school album. She had been fourteen, looking eighteen; she was twenty-four now. Her name was Billie Jean Brown. The snapshot made it hard to tell; she looked plump, an unattractive girl with colorless hair and large breasts, a pouting mouth, small eyes set close together. Her relationship to the four men in the band was uncertain and if she belonged exclusively to any one of them it had escaped Orozco's detectives. Possibly a groupie—community property, a camp-follower passed from hand to hand by the four musicians.

What sort of eerie luck had brought these five to kidnap Terry Conniston at just the right point in time to create an advantage for Oakley?

Orozco came up from the barn. The car swayed when he got in. He closed the door and wiped his face, and held one hand palm-out toward the blast of the air-conditioner. "Feels good."

"You didn't find anything."

Orozco opened his right hand. In the palm were two objects: an inch-long piece of black-rubber tubing and a folded packet of oilpaper the size of a paper matchbook.

Oakley said, "Heroin?"

"I guess."

Oakley took the oilpaper from him and had a look. "Yes."

"Dorty stuff," Orozco said. "Why you figure they lef' it behind?"

"They wouldn't have had any more use for it, would they?"

Orozco shrugged. Oakley said, "What's that other thing?"

"Strip of rubber insulation from a wire."

"Electric wire?"

"Yeah. Maybe they had ignition trouble with one of the cars."

"That tells us a lot," Oakley grumbled. "All right, let's put more men to work in Mexico. They must have left a trail."

"Cost you more money," Orozco said. "Pretty soon you'll use up enough to cover the whole damn ransom."

"That would take twenty years. A half million dollars, Diego?"

"Okay. Listen, Carl, we got to have a talk about the ranch."

"Conniston's ranch?"

"It ain't Conniston's now."

"That's right. It's mine."

"It ain't yours," Orozco murmured. "It belongs to them *chicanos.*"

†† 8

Oakley put the big car in gear and rolled into the central powder of the street. "I've got other things on my mind, Diego. Some other time."

"We been hearing that for a honnerd years—'some other time.' "

"We'll talk about it when we get this business settled." The tires crunched pebbles; the air-conditioner thrummed softly. The Cadillac gathered speed on the road going north, laying back a plume of dust. Oakley had a sour pain in his stomach. He kept wondering about the three who had survived, the three who had got away with the five hundred thousand dollars. Had they gone in a bunch or separated?

And what of Terry Conniston?

CHAPTER Two

For Mitch Baird it began not with the kidnaping but with the liquor store incident.

Mitch had been nervous all day. The band had been out of work for two weeks and he had joined only a few weeks before that, and a trio was easier to sell than a quartet, and if anybody had to be sacrificed, he'd be it. He needed a job and jobs were hard to find.

Mitch drove the old Pontiac into the shopping center lot and parked in front of the liquor store. Floyd Rymer said, "Let's just stop in a minute and get a bottle of tiger sweat." Floyd got out of the car and walked inside and because it was too hot to sit in the car Mitch followed him in.

There were two customers in the place, a man and a girl, not together. Floyd Rymer looked at each of them, looked at the clerk, and stopped to browse a Cutty Sark display, waiting for the customers to leave. Mitch looked out the window, thinking it might be a good idea to quit before he got fired. Pull up stakes and try somewhere else—San Francisco maybe, or Las Vegas.

He picked at the front of his shirt, pulling it loose from his chest and enjoying the store's frigid air-cooling. Outside it was a sultry August evening, thick with sweat. The low sun threw shards of painful brightness that drenched the shopping center in deep surrealist hues. A light traffic of air-conditioned cars, windows up, whistled along the boulevard, pulling in and out of gas stations, car lots, pizzarias, Fat Boy drive-ins. Nothing moved very fast; the hour before sunset was the worst time for driving. Tucson was laid out east to west and driving the boulevards put the blinding sun in everyone's eyes. If you weren't driving into it you were driving into fragmented reflections from the brittle chrome and plate glass that lined the strip city's thoroughfares.

One of the customers, a potbelly in a T-shirt, counted his change and wedged a six-pack of beer under his arm and left. The other customer, the plump-hipped girl with hair in curlers, was having a sotto voce conversation with the pimply counter clerk. The clerk said something gruff; the girl turned to leave. She stopped at the door and said, "Now don't be late pickin' me up, hear?"

"Sure—sure."

The girl reached for the door handle. Her glance went by Floyd Rymer, stopped, went back to him—an automatic female appraisal. Floyd had that effect on them—it annoyed Mitch, it heightened his feeling of being left out of something important. Mitch was not bad-looking; why should the girl look twice at Floyd but not at him?

Floyd's amused self-assured eyes met the girl's; the girl sucked her lip and looked awkwardly away. She hurried out, hips churning.

The clerk said, "How about the boobs on her?"

Floyd said, "Big tits make them look like cows."

"That's your opinion. How're you makin' it, Floyd?"

"Alas," said Floyd, and spread his hands before him.

"I've been expecting you to drop by."

Floyd smiled with his teeth and shaped his right hand into a mock pistol—thumb up, index finger pointed at the clerk, the other fingers curled back. "It's time, Leroy."

The clerk's acned face shifted toward Mitch: "What about him?"

"He's with me."

Mitch said, "What?"

Floyd ignored him and wagged his pistol-finger at the clerk. "Empty it out, Leroy."

⧾ 11

The clerk edged behind the cash register and hit the No Sale key. The drawer slid open with a tinkle and clack. Floyd said, "Have a look out the window, Mitch, see if anyone's coming this way."

"I don't——"

"Look, we're robbing the store. We don't want to be interrupted, do we."

"Wait a minute—we're *what?*"

"We're wasting wind," Floyd said and backed up two paces to look past Mitch through the window. "Go ahead, Leroy, it'll be all right."

The clerk shook open a paper bag and scooped cash into it from the register drawer. He pushed the drawer shut, furtive in haste; handed the bag to Floyd and stepped swiftly away.

"How much?" Floyd asked.

"About seven hundred." Leroy bit a fingernail. "I don't guess you'll forget what to do with my share."

Floyd gave him a dry look and said after a moment, "You remember what we looked like?"

"There was three of them, Officer. This great big guy had the gun. They had nylon stockings or something over their faces but I'm sure they was Mexicans. I seen them take off in a green pickup truck."

"Stick to that." Floyd rolled the paper bag shut and walked toward the door. "Come on, Mitch."

Mitch drove with his head hunched, squinting under the lowered sun visor. The windshield was frosted with dust and the road was hard to see. Against his back the seat cover felt squirmy with sweat.

Floyd said, "You really ought to wash this heap."

They drove past a future slum of sleazy crackerbox development ranch-houses with weedy yards. Floyd said, "Stay inside the speed limit, my fine buffoon. Hang a left there and take us downtown."

Mitch manhandled the old Pontiac around the corner. Floyd looked at his face. "Lose something, Mitch?"

"I don't suppose you're going to break down and tell me what that was all about."

"What do you think it was all about?"

"You made a deal with Leroy to stage that phony robbery and split with him. But why bring me into it? What do you want a witness for?"

"Maybe just to prove how much I trust you," Floyd said. But a block farther on he added gently, "You're not a witness, Mitch —you're an accessory." He smiled.

"What the hell do you mean?"

"You helped me rob the place and you're driving the getaway car."

"For Christ's sake I didn't even *know* about it."

Floyd turned sideways in the seat and laid his left arm along the back of it. "If I'd told you about it beforehand would you have gone with me?"

"No. Yes. Christ, I don't know, but at least you could've given me a chance to think about it first."

"Aeah. Well there are a few things you do all right, Mitch, but thinking isn't one of them."

Mitch closed his mouth. There was no point arguing when Floyd was in one of his superior moods. Mitch spared him a brief sidewise glance. Floyd looked relaxed, one arm crook'd on the seat back, the other propping up the roof, elbow on sill. Mitch said, "We could get in a lot of trouble."

"Not if you keep your mouth shut."

"Is that why you brought me in on it, to make sure I'd keep my mouth shut?"

Floyd made no answer of any kind. It was as if he hadn't heard. But he said in a patient tone, "Look, we needed money, now we've got money."

"A few hundred bucks isn't worth five years in Florence."

"You ought to know about that."

"I haven't been in any trouble since I got out. I want to keep it like that."

The street dipped under a railroad overpass and Mitch leaned forward to see into the dimness underneath. When they emerged on the downtown side the street narrowed between austere new high-rise buildings and they inched forward in traffic clotted like blood. Mitch said, "When I asked you for a job I told you I'd done a few months' time. You said that was all right so I thought you were doing me a favor, but I'm getting the feeling you hired me *because* I'd done time, not in spite of it."

"I don't know what you're complaining about. You'll never make a living playing that guitar of yours—if you've got any talent it must be in your grandmother's name."

"That's not true and you know it."

"I do?"

"I hold up my end. I'm the best you've ever had in this third-rate band."

"To be sure," Floyd murmured. "But that does us a fat lot of good when we can't get booked."

A light turned green and they started to move ahead. Floyd said, "Turn left up ahead and start looking for a phone booth. I want to make a call."

Mitch made the turn into the southbound boulevard. It was a woebegone strip of lumberyards, motels and bars. There was a tight string of intersection gas stations, pennants flapping, bitterly engaged in a furious price war.

Floyd said, "Listen, there are millions of musicians around— do you really want to spend the rest of your life picking at a guitar in fifty-cent bars? How old are you?"

"Twenty-three."

"Grade B jobs for Grade B wages. All you can get, Mitch. You want to eat beans the rest of your life? You want to get old and retire on your union pension? I don't."

"It's better than prison."

"Only the stupid ones end up there."

"Here's your phone booth."

The sun was going down fast; neon signs were lighting up. Mitch stopped by the roadside booth and Floyd got out, leaving the car door open. He didn't shut the phone-booth door and Mitch could hear the coins drop in the phone. After a minute Floyd spoke into the mouthpiece:

"This is Rymer. I've got a car that needs fixing. . . . No, I'm afraid it won't move at all. I'd like to have the mechanic come over here and look at it. I'm at the Twenty-first place, same as last time. . . . Sure, you've done some work for me before. It's a 1949 Studebaker. . . . Yes, right away—say ten minutes."

Floyd hung up and got back into the car. "Let's go down Twenty-first."

"You haven't got any 1949 Studebaker."

"Think of that," Floyd said.

Don't get uptight, he told himself. *Don't bust your mind until you find out what the bastard's up to.*

It was a dingy maculose street. Shanties of corrugated metal, junkyards, here and there a squat adobe bar isolated by dusty yards. Floyd said, "That one on the corner under the Schlitz sign."

A wheelless Model-A Ford stood on bricks in the vacant lot beside the bar. Mitch pulled into the dirt yard by the billboard; dust hung around the car when Floyd got out. The door chunked shut and Floyd leaned his shaggy head in the window. "Come in with me."

"What for?"

Floyd came around the car and opened Mitch's door.

"You going to rob another till?"

"Relax. Nothing like that."

Twilight fanned gray and pink across the clouds. Mitch got out of the car and followed Floyd into the bar. It was dim and pungent, lit by blue bulbs and beer ads and redolent of stale beer and tobacco smoke. Four or five patrons—Mexican laborers and an old carpenter in overalls—sat on bar stools hunched over lonely drinks. The gaudy jukebox's heavy speakers pulsed with the loud bass notes of a rock and roll tune.

Floyd propped himself on a stool, one leg stretched to the floor, and ordered two beers. He looked at the clock. Mitch watched the bartender draw beers and bring them forward. A dumpy woman came into the place, looked at nobody, went straight through to the bathroom at the back.

Floyd took a slow sip from his beer, yawned, and got off the stool. "Come on."

"What?"

Floyd started toward the back of the room. Baffled, Mitch

followed him into the rancid yellow dimness of the bathroom.

Floyd let him through and shut the door. The dumpy woman stood just outside the toilet booth; she had a plain round face, a bulbous blob of a nose, a little sweetheart rose on the collar of her cotton dress. Her eyes expressed tired contempt. "I hope you ain't wasting my time because I don't do business on the cuff."

Floyd unrolled the paper bag and took out a fistful of cash. The woman watched with polite bovine interest. "You've just said the magic word," she said. "How much stuff do you want?"

Mitch glanced at the door; he felt irritated and apprehensive. He looked at the woman and at Floyd. Floyd stood motionless, the smoke of a cigarette making a vague suspended cloud before his cold face. "Enough to take care of a big habit for a week or so," he said.

"Ten pops?"

"Make it fifteen."

"Cost you ten apiece," she said with no show of emotion. "A hundred and fifty."

Floyd counted it off in twenties and tens, squared up the sheaf and put the rest back in the paper bag. He handed the bag to Mitch. The woman reached for the money but Floyd drew back. "Where's the stuff?"

"I'll get it to you."

"No," Floyd said.

"You don't trust me?" She smiled a little. "Look, my mother didn't raise any stupid kids. I'm not going to walk into a place like this with that much junk in my handbag."

"Then get it."

The woman pinched her lower lip between two fingers. Her studious gaze shifted from Floyd to Mitch; several beats went by before she said, "You're not users, either one of you. How do I know you're not cops?"

"We're not cops," Floyd said dryly.

Uncertainty quivered in her eyes; finally Floyd smiled and shook his head and said, "Use your head. Did I turn you in last time?"

"All right, all right. It's outside in the car. Follow me out in a minute."

When she left the bathroom Floyd made no move to follow her. The door squeaked shut and Mitch said immediately, "I didn't know your brother had a habit *that* big. How long can he last like that?"

"How should I know?"

"Don't you care at all?"

Floyd just looked at him. There was no reading his face. Mitch said, "Why in hell don't you send him in for a cure?"

"He's had the cure twice," Floyd muttered, and turned, his mind on something else. He washed his hands at the sink and dried them on a paper towel. "All right," he said, and went out.

Mitch paid for the beers on the way out. They found the dumpy woman waiting in a dusty new station wagon. She had the engine running, the lights switched off, the door shut and the window open. It was getting dark fast. She handed Floyd a small package and Mitch saw Floyd turn over the money—it disappeared immediately inside her dress, which was probably where she'd had the goods hidden all along. She pulled the gear lever into reverse. Floyd said in a mild way, "If this stuff's no good I'll know where to find you."

The station wagon backed out and swung around into the street before she turned the lights on. It fishtailed away with a scudding of back tires chattering for traction. Floyd coughed and batted dust away. "That's what happens when you give petty authority to scum like that. Let's go."

Mitch got in the car and started it up and they drove through the raw, neon-lighted streets without talk. He was thinking there were a lot of things about Floyd that didn't make sense. Floyd's junkie brother couldn't play the bass fiddle for sour apples—if Floyd had had a good bass man he could have put together a good band a long time ago. Georgie had a $150-a-week habit: he was nothing but a liability. Yet Mitch had just seen Floyd take stupid risks for Georgie's sake. Floyd was not a stupid man. It didn't quite add up. Brotherly love did not fit into Floyd's image.

They reached the freeway interchange and turned southeast on the superhighway. Floyd checked his watch and said, "Pull over to the shoulder when you get a chance."

"What for?"

"Yours not to reason why, Mitch."

He rolled the Pontiac off the roadway and crunched to a stop. "Well?"

"Just wait until I tell you to go. I want to see something. Leave the lights on."

Mitch curbed his tongue and settled back, fished out a cigarette and punched the dashboard lighter. The lights of cars passed them at speed. There was nothing much to look at—tall gooseneck highway lights, a few truck stops clustered around the interchange half a mile ahead, scrubby desert crowding the road shoulders, the Rincon Mountains vague in the falling night. The day's heat was dissipating fast.

Floyd sat twisted around, squinting through the back window. Mitch made a face and pressed the red lighter to his cigarette. Floyd was looking at his watch again and Mitch started to say something but Floyd cut him off: "Shut up. It's just about time."

"Time for what, for Christ's sake?"

There was no response. Mitch drew smoke deep into his lungs and frowned. He had had enough; it was definitely time to quit. He didn't like Floyd and what was the point of hanging onto a job that offered no work and no pay? He would pack his things as soon as they got back to the motel. It wouldn't be wise to mention it to the others, particularly to Floyd; no, he would just pack and go.

Floyd stiffened. Mitch followed the direction of his glance and saw a red sports car come up fast from behind, passing under the street light; it swept past and droned away in the beams of Mitch's headlights. He had a glimpse of a vivid, pretty girl at the wheel.

Floyd said, "We can go now."

"Who was that?"

"Her name, my learned friend, is Terry Conniston. She takes an evening summer course four nights a week at the University and drives home about this time every night, home being the Conniston ranch down near Sonoita."

"Girl friend of yours?"

"We've never met," Floyd said.

"Then what is it?"

"Contain your impatience, there's a good boy. Let's get home."

Intent on his own plans to break away, Mitch didn't press it. He flipped the cigarette out the vent window and angled the car back onto the freeway. Within a few minutes they turned off and rolled into the gravel parking yard of a truckers' café. There were a few dead letters in the neon Modern Motel sign. When they had lost the last nightclub gig they had sought the cheapest rooms available, and here they were.

Floyd picked up the sack of liquor-store money and the packet of dope—twin handfuls of evidential explosive—and they went around the side of the café to the outside staircase that hung uneasily to the flimsy side of the building. Through the kitchen's back door Mitch could see a fat Mexican woman in an apron slapping corn tortillas from arm to arm. The place was flyblown and filthy. The stairs creaked when Mitch put his weight on them.

The upstairs door let them into a long narrow hall, seamy and waterstained, lit by one yellow forty-watt bulb. Mitch stopped at the door to his room and said vaguely, "I'll see you," and watched Floyd go on toward his brother's room; Floyd said over his shoulder:

"We'll get something to eat in a little while."

"Sure." Mitch went inside and shut the door behind him. He looked around the tiny room without expression. It smelled of cheap disinfectant and the washbasin and cracked toilet-bowl had yellow stains from the dripping erosion of years. The room had one plain kitchen chair with chipped offwhite paint and a sagging bed redolent of hasty sex, loveless furtive perversions, tired-eyed whores. Once when he was seventeen he had spent part of a night with a high school girl in a room like this. It had been awkward and frantic and unhappy.

He heaved his suitcase onto the bed and threw his meager belongings into it. After that he sat down in the chair and smoked; he would wait and leave after the others were all asleep.

He could see himself in the corner-cracked mirror over the

basin. It surprised him how boyish he still looked—the youthful broad face still not far beyond a careless ease of smiling. It was hard to understand how he had possibly come to this dreary place in his life. He had always had the best of his world: he was athletic, smart, attractive to girls, the son of decent middle-class parents from an ordinary suburban town. He was no hippie, no rebel. But in his pleasant youth he had never been tested. His splendid health and brain and surroundings had let him assume that things would always come easily.

His sophomore college year had ambushed him—a few too many beer parties and rehearsals and band gigs at fraternity houses, and he had walked into the physics final exam knowing with sudden hollow fear that he was not going to pass. And the tough old Lit professor had failed him for spelling mistakes. Flunked two courses out of five—that had put him out.

His father and mother had tried to be kind and understanding but through the brave pretense Mitch could see their crushed bitter disappointment. His father had got him a job in the real estate office. Mitch had tried but he couldn't face them every day seeing what they were thinking: twenty-one and a failure. He had run away, baffled and hurt. He would become a success, build up a band of his own, make records and money. He joined a band in New Mexico, swingers, and then had come the months in jail, and now this.

He supposed he ought to start thinking about where he would go. To another town, maybe, check in with the musicians' union local and see if anyone was hiring. He had enough for a bus ticket to Salt Lake or Las Vegas. Then too he could always wire his father for money and go home to Cleveland. But that would be admitting he had failed again. He didn't want that. He didn't want to say a word to them until he could show them he had made a success of himself.

He crushed the cigarette out underfoot, got up and took the cased electric guitar from the corner and put it on the bed beside the suitcase. That was everything he owned. The sight of it sagging on the dilapidated bed turned his sense of dismal depression to fear, a sudden lonely sense of panic. A dry taste like brass on his tongue, an urgency in his groin. He remembered how, when he had been twelve, his father had taken him duck-hunting on the remote north shore of the lake. In the cold wet dawn his father had left him in a blind and moved away to a farther blind beyond earshot or sight. For hours Mitch had been convinced his father had got lost, forgotten where he was, forgotten about him entirely. He had felt the terror of being lost and alone.

He jumped when his door latched open. Floyd Rymer, in the door, gave him a dry look and said, "Know what you need?"

"A lock on my door?"

Floyd started to speak but then his eye fell on the cases on the bed. "Well, now,"—sarcastic—"what's this?"

Mitch said reluctantly, "I'm clearing out."

"Just like that?"

He needed to talk fast. "Look, we're not doing each other any good, are we? I'm just a fifth wheel the way things are—you can get bookings a lot quicker if you cut back to three men and anyway I'm getting sick of this hot country. I think I'll head north and see what I can pick up around Vegas or Tahoe."

"You won't have any luck. It's a slow summer everywhere— they're all buying jukeboxes and Muzak because it's cheaper than live musicians."

"I'll take my chances, I guess."

"Then take them with me, Mitch."

"Why?"

"Believe me, you'll do far better with me."

"It doesn't look that way from here. Anyway I'd think you'd be anxious to get rid of me."

Floyd said, softly so he would know it was important, "I need somebody around here with a level head on his shoulders."

Floyd pushed the door shut, hooked the chair over to him and sat down cowboy fashion, legs astraddle the back of the chair and arms folded across the top. "Besides, you know too much. Suppose you get picked up for vagrancy and decide to earn brownie points by turning me in? I can't very well afford to let you do that, now, can I."

"I'd have to implicate myself to turn you in. With my record that's hardly likely."

Floyd had a dry quizzical smile. "Do you want to know why I pulled off that liquor-store thing?"

"Does it matter?"

"Yes, to me. I did it because I wanted to make sure it would work. I wanted to be sure I could get away with something like that. And I wanted to see which way you'd jump."

"So?"

"It was a rehearsal," Floyd said. "A practice scrimmage to warm us up for a bigger ball game. Is that a spark of interest I see in your eye? That's good because I'll need your help to pull it off."

"I don't think I even want to hear about it."

"Of course you do. If you don't find out what I'm talking about your curiosity won't ever let you alone." Floyd got up abruptly, shoved the chair away and reached for the door. "Come on, Mitch," he said, in a voice gone suddenly flat and hard.

As he started toward the door, it occurred vaguely to Mitch that never once in his life had he wanted anything, or wanted *not* to do anything, badly enough to fight for it.

He didn't fight Floyd. He went with him down the hall to Georgie's room.

CHAPTER **Three**

They were all gathered in Georgie's room. Mitch thought it
looked like a cell meeting in a lunatic asylum.

Georgie Rymer sat curled on the far corner of the bed, a tense
gaunt shape in the shadows. He wore a candy-striped shirt and
a necktie made of a raccoon tail. He had long hair, girl-long,
down to his shoulders. Georgie's upper jaw poked forward, giving his mouth the look of a gopher with two big front teeth
showing. The trivial moustache on his upper lip failed to give
him the toughened appearance it was intended to provide.
Georgie was blowing his nose when Mitch came in with Floyd.
He didn't look up. He had an unbreakable facial apathy that
indicated he was high on a recent dose, half freaked out.

Theodore Luke stood close against the girl, frowning, earnestly scratching his buttock with stubborn determination. He
wore only a T-shirt and drawers; he was a hulking brute with
thick hair on his arms and legs. The back of his head was flat and
he had let his hair grow very long not because it was the fashion
of the moment but because it helped conceal his face. Theodore's face was distorted and crippled—asymmetrical and
cauliflowered where plastic surgeons had grafted on an ugly
imitation in place of an ear he had lost in an automobile wreck
at the age of seven. His right eyelid was partially paralyzed; it
tended to droop—he couldn't keep it altogether open or altogether closed, not even when he was asleep. It revealed an

opaque, gray-clouded eye, blind and not coordinated with its mate. The face had made it inevitable that Theodore learn to be a deadly vicious fighter and he had learned early in childhood how to hate murderously. But from some amazing reservoir of talent Theodore had dredged the rare ability to play the drums softly and with intricate delicacy.

Right by Theodore stood Billie Jean Brown, leaning against the wall with one hand clutched in her hair. She was sensuous and spider-waisted. The sweep of her eyebrows was emphasized in dark pencil but her face was nondescript, pouting and dull. She was a creature of sensation. Her feet were flat and her breasts were just beginning to sag; she wore nothing under her thin print dress. Mitch doubted she owned any underclothes.

Theodore crowded close against her and put his hand inside the front of Billie Jean's dress. Her eyes closed and she made small gutteral sounds.

Mitch made a face and looked away. Floyd was beside him, just inside the door, standing the way he often stood on the bandstand when he sang: relaxed like a crooner, one hand in the pocket, a lidded lazy smile, casual glance roving the audience. There was no denying Floyd possessed a magnetic charisma. He had the grace and self-confidence of a decathlon champion. Just now, amused by what he saw, he seemed in no hurry to call the group to order. Billie Jean and Theodore were oblivious to anything but themselves; the girl's dumpling face was closed up happily. One hand tangled in her hair, the other propped impudently on her hip, she surged her plump young breast up full into Theodore's palm. Sweat rolled freely along Theodore's grotesque face, filled with a rubbery leer of sensual pleasure. Moving languorously, Billie Jean slipped her hand into the fly of his shorts.

Floyd slammed the door. "All right, don't go ape."

Theodore looked up drowsily. "Ain't she a pistol?"

Floyd said, "We've got business to discuss."

"You want to see us do it? Right here standing up against the wall?"

"I wouldn't buy a ticket," Floyd said. "Now cut it out, both of you. I don't want to have to repeat myself again."

Billie Jean pushed her lips out and withdrew her hand. Aroused, Theodore reached for her but Billie Jean twisted away; she said, "Not now."

"To hell with him," Theodore growled.

Floyd moved two steps into the room. Billie Jean looked quickly, anxiously at him. She said, "Not now, Theodore. Don't you remember how Floyd beat up on that trucker in Amarillo? He was twice your size and he must've been laid up for a month."

Theodore dropped his arms to his sides, sucking air like a grounded fish. Floyd said mildly, "Go sit down and breathe through your nose."

Theodore moved grudgingly, sat down on the edge of the bed and put a finger in his nose. Georgie on the bed was slowly uncoiling from his curled-up reverie. Sprawling as if boneless, he blinked pale-eyed in sulky silence.

"All right," Floyd said. "Gentlemen, I solicit your attention. Theodore, stop picking your nose. Wipe that vacant bewildered look off your face and pay attention."

"Me pay attention? What about the hophead? What about Georgie?"

Hearing his name, Georgie lifted his head. "Time is it now?"

Theodore snapped, "That's the howmanyest time you've asked me that?"

Georgie rubbed his face. "Okay, go ahead, I'm listening."

Floyd moved his glance deliberately from face to face. Mitch glared at him. Floyd said, "Prosperity is just around the corner, boys. It's time we change our station in life before we end up with holes in our shoes like my benighted old man, God rot his memory."

Our old man," said Georgie.

"I stand corrected; your point is well taken." Floyd's glance whipped down the room to him and there was something remote and vicious in it. "Georgie and I," he murmured, "do not intend to end up like our old man."

Theodore said, "You got us a job, huh?"

"In a manner of speaking. A very large job. What we're going to do is pull off a little extra-legal caper—a statutory offense if you will. We're going to borrow a rich man's daughter for a little while and the rich man's going to pay us to get her back."

Mitch stared at him, not believing. Billie Jean said, "You talking about kidnaping somebody?"

Theodore's head swiveled. "Kidnap? Is that what you said?"

Floyd observed, "Theodore, you're incredibly adept at grasping the obvious as soon as someone spells it out for you."

Mitch said, "Aagh," in disgust and backed up against the wall, hooking his hands in his pockets. "You're putting us on."

"I'm putting you onto a fat share of a half million dollars," Floyd answered. It was a quiet snarl and he let it fall into the room and lie among them, stirring sluggishly.

It was a while before anyone spoke.

"A half million dollars?" Georgie said. "Five hundred thousand dollars?"

Theodore said, "Who do we have to grab for that kind of money? Who's got that kind of money?"

"Earle Conniston. As in Conniston Oil, Conniston Construction, and Conniston Aerospace Industries. He lives on a secluded estate he pleases to call a ranch about forty miles south of here. He has a daughter who's very dear to his heart because his only son was killed last year and she's all he's got left."

Billie Jean was rubbing her palms on her hips. "That's a lot of money, Floyd."

Mitch shook his head in exasperation and heard Theodore say, "Yeah, she's right. Nobody's got that much cash lying around and you can't exactly ask the man for a check."

"Theodore, you hear the words but you don't hear the music, do you? Earle Conniston's a *very* rich man. Taking half a million from him is like taking dimes from a man who makes dollars. He'll never miss it—not a tenth as much as he'll miss his daughter."

A broken interval of silent time stretched by. In the end, excited, Theodore bounced to his feet. "Sure. Why don't we? Hell, all that money? Man, Floyd, you are something else."

Georgie sat up on the bed, drew his knees up and wrapped his thin arms around them. "I don't know, Floyd, I mean, *kid*-naping——"

"And just how do *you* expect to pay for that habit of yours?"

"Habit?" Georgie's eyes wandered weakly away. "I took the cure, Floyd, I can take the stuff or leave it—Christ sake, I'm not a *junkie* or something. And if I like a jolt now and then it don't take any half million dollars—I mean, you go out and kidnap somebody, they lock you up for keeps."

"Not if they never find out who you are," Floyd said. His voice clacked abruptly: "All right, you've all had your say, now I'll put in my fifty-one percent worth. We abduct the girl tomorrow night and then we arrange to collect the money from Daddy Warbucks. I've got everything laid out——"

"Wait a minute." Mitch, finding his tongue, stepped forward. "Wait just a minute. You can't expect us to go along with a crazy thing like that. Even Georgie knows better—lock you up for keeps is exactly what they'll do. Anyhow what do you need all that money for?"

"I'm going to paper my living room walls with it," Floyd said darkly. "What do you think I'm going to do with it? Are you trying to tell me you can't use a hundred thousand dollars, Mitch?"

"Not in jail. Not in the gas chamber. They still have capital punishment in Arizona."

"Nobody gets arrested. The way I have it planned nobody will even see our faces. They'll never find us out. It's perfect. It can't miss. The girl drives home the same route every night from school. She leaves the freeway at Mountain View and takes State Highway Eighty-three south to her daddy's ranch. It's a twenty-mile stretch of the loneliest mountain road in the world. We pick her up there tomorrow night and we take her to a place I've already reconnoitered—plenty of room to hide her and us and the cars. They won't find us even if they use X-rays. It's one of those old ghost towns, nobody ever comes around the place in the summer. Fifteen miles from the nearest paved road. You can see a long way from the rooftops—we can spot cars or helicopters before they get within ten miles of us."

Floyd went on, talking smoothly. It was the hypnotic confidence of his baritone voice more than the words themselves that always made it hard to dispute him. He had an oracular air of sincerity and omniscience; he made any thought of argument against him seem foolish and demeaning.

He said, "Tomorrow morning we'll sell the Pontiac and steal a car that can't be traced to us. I've already fixed us up with a lineman's telephone rig—there's a phone line at the main road fifteen miles north of Soledad and we can splice right into the cross-country line. We'll use electronic whistle codes to dial Conniston's phone direct, through the automatic switchboard— it'll take the phone company months to figure out where we were calling from. They can't trace calls to a phone that doesn't exist. We'll only hook it in when we're using it—we disconnect after each call. Now, we'll stock up on food and water tomorrow afternoon. . . ."

His voice droned on, flat and authoritarian, leaving nothing open to challenge. When he stopped it was Theodore who spoke first:

"You sure thought of everything."

"Everything," Floyd agreed. "Nothing happens that I don't want to happen. There'll be no unnecessary frills, no gimmicks. It's a simple job. I've got the ransom drop worked out to the last detail. There'll be no traps and no way for them to see who picks up the money."

As he spoke Floyd kept his eyes level on Mitch. Mitch felt cornered. He said, "They'll bring the FBI in right off."

"What if they do? They won't find us. Nobody will—nobody can."

"Nuts," Mitch said. "It's ridiculous. You're not even talking about kidnaping a little kid. The girl's grown up."

"Are you suggesting the five of us can't handle one seventeen-year-old girl?" Floyd aimed a slow wink at Theodore, who uttered a penetrating rasp of a laugh.

Mitch looked at the others, suppressing a sense of panic. He saw no help anywhere. Georgie's eyes weren't tracking quite right but even so he was pointedly avoiding Mitch's gaze. Theodore and Billie Jean moved forward and fixed themselves to Floyd. Dark sweat-circles stained the armpits of Theodore's T-shirt. Mitch felt his face color under Theodore's ugly one-eyed stare.

Floyd smiled and reached out suddenly, gripping Mitch's

arm. The steel fingers bit into Mitch's flesh, the thumb casually working cartilage against bone. Mitch burst out in a gray sweat. Floyd said softly, "I need you to make it work, Mitch."

"I—"

"You'll do it. You didn't like grinding your life away in school, did you? You don't want to starve on the beer circuit, do you? It's the best opportunity anybody ever offered you."

"I never did anything like that in my life," Mitch said weakly. "I never even thought about it before."

"It's a me-first world, Mitch. You take what you can grab."

Theodore said, "If Floyd says we need you then you do like he says. Or we turn out your lights, see?"

Floyd turned his arm loose. Mitch rubbed the pain abstractedly. He wasn't looking at anybody. He could hear the ragged sawing of Theodore's breathing.

He said, "All right—all right. Hell, why not?"

Floyd smiled. "That's the way." Then, turning away, he stopped to look at Mitch once more, and asked merrily, "Am I not a son of a bitch, Mitch?" He laughed.

Mitch nodded with little jerks of his head. He knew what he was going to do anyway. He was going to get loose of them the first chance he saw and make a run for it.

CHAPTER **Four**

Earle Conniston's ranch sprawled across a third of a million scrub-grass acres of valley and foothills. A hand-crank gasoline pump stood at the end of the landing strip opposite the wind-sock. Coming in an hour ago, Carl Oakley had had to buzz the strip twice to chase half a dozen white-face steers off the grass runway. He had parked his Cessna beside Conniston's big Lear Jet and hitched a ride with a Mexican cowboy in a jeep loaded with rock-salt to the main house a quarter of a mile from the airfield. The house was boomerang-shaped, elaborate and Moorish, built of high-quality adobe with the archways of a shady galleried verandah running the length of it. The house was shaded by a copse of tall heavy cottonwood trees, planted twenty-five years ago and earnestly watered twice a week.

Twenty-three years ago Oakley, the young GI-Bill lawyer, had met Earle Conniston, the thirty-five-year-old businessman. A knee-injury from college football had kept Conniston out of the wartime army and by 1947 Conniston had built a small war-surplus junk business into the beginnings of a cartel. Conniston in those days had had a glittering smile, a quick glibness, a pushing dogged ambition. He was chest-combingly masculine, big-shouldered with thick hair on his arms and legs, and eyes that needed to look at things only once: he could absorb hundreds of details with a glance. He was big enough to seem oversized, as craggy as Rushmore even at thirty-five. He wasn't ugly but he was huge and rough; he had the important look of austere dignity that prevented people from slapping his back or elbow-nudging his ribs—he always got quick service from waitresses and desk clerks.

Oakley had met him in a poker game. By 1949 he had won two lawsuits for Conniston and made himself indispensable to the rising buccaneer. He had appraised Conniston of the tax advantages of cattle ownership and scouted the Southwest until he had found the right property at the right price. Eighteen years ago, on Oakley's advice, Conniston had bought this ranch.

Since the end of the war in Korea Earle Conniston had divided and multiplied like a financial amoeba. He was a tough grizzly and, fittingly, his powerful wealth came right out of the guts of the world—oil from Texas, steel from Michigan, steamships prowling the oceans, lumber and pulp mills in northern California, trucks on highways and tractors on vast company-owned farms and ranches from Florida to Montana.

Oakley had traveled the whole route with him. His personal fortunes had massed, the result of abundant salary and generous bonuses; if remaining a mere salaried employee disturbed him he gave no indication of it. Conniston never offered partnership and Oakley never demanded it. But the intricate convolutions of the Conniston empire were kept in balance mainly by the cleverness of Carl Oakley's brain; Oakley had seen to it that he became the vital cornerstone of the structure. They were friends; they respected each other's talents like two generals, one of whom commanded plans and the other operations; yet it was an alert relationship, honed by mutual distrust. Sometimes in fits of black humor Oakley saw himself as Conniston's Rasputin. He lacked the power to displace the czar on the throne; yet he had far too much damaging knowledge ever to be expendable.

Today Oakley had come down from Phoenix in two hours, been met by Conniston's third wife, Louise, and shown to the largest of the guest bedrooms, where he stripped and showered in preparation for the long afternoon's intense conference. He scratched his belly and stood in front of the mirror with his lips peeled back, inspecting his strong teeth and thinking idly that perhaps it was about time he got married. The decades of sybaritic bachelorhood were beginning to wear on him. A little flab starting to show up around the waist and shoulders: it might be best to find a marriageable woman before he lost his hair and his looks. Getting into slacks and sport shirt, he ran down the catalogue of eligible divorcees and spinsters, made a face and went out into the thick-walled corridor.

The house was cooled by a seven-ton air-conditioning plant concealed in oleander bushes beyond the swimming pool; the corridor was noiselessly cool in spite of the hundred-degree heat outside. Oakley's moccasins flipflopped along the carpeted hundred feet of hallway to the huge front room, where Louise stood petulantly arranging flowers in a vase. Either she hadn't seen him or she was pretending to be unaware of his approach. She moved around the vase, inspecting it from various angles, moving slowly because it was more graceful; almost everything Louise did was studied. She was only twenty-eight. Conniston had met her two years ago in New York, shortly after the divorce from his second wife. Louise had been a showgirl-turned-actress; in some ways Oakley knew more about her than Conniston did, since it had been his job to run down her past when Conniston became serious enough about her to warrant the investigation. She had worked her way up from modeling runway to off-Broadway stage, done a few television commercials and been tapped by a producer to play the ingenue opposite Henry Fonda in a bit of Broadway fluff that ran seven weeks. That was where Conniston had seen her; he had invaded backstage country, breached her dressing room and rushed her like a football running-back.

Conniston had the customary tycoon's desire for younger women; he also liked talent in his women. His first wife, Terry's mother, had been a violinist; when her desire to return to her career had crossed Conniston's need for an ornament and social hostess the marriage had cracked up. The second wife had been a painter; her work was as vivid and flashy as her person. Conniston had paid an art professor to write a book about her painting but even that hadn't helped get the canvases into respectable galleries; her one and only critical notice in the *New York Times* had said, "As for Mrs. Conniston's work, aside from a certain flamboyant gusto, it can only be described as a mediocre example of the neo-excretionist school." That marriage had soured for much the same reasons that caused today's rigid expression on Louise Conniston's sensuous face.

Louise had a tall solid body, trimmed by daily workouts against a ballet exercise bar. She had thick tawny hair and animated, amorous features. Her large eyes were passionate; her expressions had a wide and subtle range of colors which at first tended to obscure the rather ordinary mind beyond. She had a honey tan and superb long legs; she wore a vinyl miniskirt and a sleeveless blouse that clung electrically to her velvet curves. Oakley watched her pirouette slowly to face him.

"Oh—Carl. I didn't know you were there." She didn't look at all startled.

He said, "You're looking lovely, as always."

Her smile had just the right degree of rehearsed demureness. It faded quickly and she said, "I suppose you'll have him locked up with you in there all afternoon and half the night."

"We've got quite a bit to go over," he conceded. "Have to pack a lot into these short trips of mine down here. Why? You seem upset."

"It's only——" she began, and stopped. She tipped her head to one side, a little-girl pose, and absently fingered a flower petal above the vase. "He just came back from Washington last Saturday. I hardly have any time at all alone with him any more." Clearly it wasn't what she had started out to say.

"I'll try to cut it short," Oakley said, more out of politeness than honesty. "It's up to him, you know."

"I know," she said; the curl of her lip seemed, for a change, involuntary. Her eyes were still averted.

"Well," Oakley said, and turned toward the study door.

"Wait."

He stopped and looked at her. She said, "Carl, you knew his other wives, Dorothy and Marianne."

Whatever was coming, he thought he didn't want to hear it. He said as much, or began to: "I don't think it's any of my——"

"No. I have to ask you something. Those marriages, Carl why did they fall apart?"

"In twenty-five words or less? You know I can't give you a simple answer to a question like that. Maybe I don't even know the real answers. Why don't you ask Earle?"

"Was it," she pressed, "—neglect?"

"Neglect? By whom? What kind of crazy ideas have you got?"

Her face changed. She turned half away, hiding her eyes from him, and muttered so that he barely caught the words, "It's been getting worse for months. He just shuts me out. He never even says good night to me any more. What can I do? Tell me what to do, Carl."

"Why ask me?" he replied, more harshly than he had intended, but her act angered him—he was sure now it was an act after all and he disliked the sordid presumptions it implied, that he was nothing more than a gullible audience for her histrionics. He had no idea what motivated the theatrics but he did know her well enough to be sure she would never unburden herself to him so casually if there weren't something hidden behind it.

She seemed unaffected by his peremptory remark; she only said in a small voice, "What's going to happen, Carl?"

He shook his head obstinately. "I'm a lawyer, not an oracle. Look, I apologize for snapping at you. But I learned a long time ago to stay out of other people's domestic tangles. It's not my field of law. Talk to a marriage counselor. Better yet, why not talk to Earle?"

"I have. He just doesn't listen. It's as if I'm not even there."

"I'm sorry," he said lamely, angry at Conniston for being so clumsy (if she was telling the truth), equally angry at Louise for trying to involve him. He reached for the knob of the study door.

She said absently, "He's not in there. He's in the office."

He shot a quick glance at her, which she didn't notice; she was bent over the flowers as if holding back tears. He pushed back the momentary impulse to leave the room rudely and quickly; instead he crossed the room with brisk strides and put an arm across her shoulders. "Come on, now. Come on."

"Never mind. I'm all right. You're right—it's not your problem and I had no right dragging you into it."

He patted her arm, feeling foolish as he did so. Her flesh was soft and warm; his carnal instincts stirred, he stepped away from her. She lifted her face toward him and stared, unblinking; her breasts rose and fell with her breathing. If it was a pose it was effective. But if she meant him to draw implications from it they were implications he couldn't afford to explore. A bit of a smile flashed briefly across his cheeks and he shook his head at her with more irony than displeasure. Unable to think of anything useful to say, he walked slowly away. Her voice, pitched low, followed him to the door:

"If you get a chance see if you can find out what I've done that's offended him."

"Sure." He went back through the cool corridor to the office and knocked. There was a clack and a buzz—Conniston had an electric button under his desk which automatically unlocked the door; the cork-lined office was his working sanctum. When Oakley stepped inside he was on his guard: in Earle Conniston's house the study was for friends and the office was for pure business. So it wasn't to be a casual afternoon.

A row of brown filing cabinets stood at attention along one cork-paneled wall. There was a Utrillo and a small blue Picasso; otherwise the room was bare of decoration. A scatter of leather chairs; a sound-absorbent carpet, plain beige; the big man's desk, dominant, kidney-shaped walnut.

Conniston was scowling, talking into one of the phones. His attention whipped down the room to Oakley; he nodded. Oakley pushed the door shut with his heel. Conniston's deep baritone growled at the phone:

"Yes. Might be important fact. . . . Then juice up the accounting—feel they aren't depreciating things fast enough. What about Raiford? . . . Why not? They've all got hands out for the sugar tit, haven't they? Don't tell me Bob Raiford's developed sudden attack of acute integrity. Doesn't fit. Christ, in the old days you could buy a senator with pocket money—now got to give the bastards TV station and two newspapers. . . . Well, then, get to work on him. What do you mean, when? Get started two hours ago."

Clearly it was a long conversation, only half completed. A

kind of dull peace settled on Oakley and he let Conniston's phone talk go by. He put a cigar in his mouth but didn't light it and after a few minutes, with Conniston's voice droning on, he left the chair and went past Conniston to stand at the window and look out across the flagstoned back patio. Fifty feet from the house was a lawn fountain, a baroque relic Conniston had picked up in Europe; it resembled a bird bath for buzzards, to Oakley's austere way of thinking. Just beyond was the swimming pool built of cement and tile and money. Someone was splashing in the pool; he couldn't make out the swimmer's identity against the sun-glare and cascading shards of water. But within a minute or two the swimmer climbed out of the pool and reached for a towel—Terry Conniston.

She moved lightly and quickly—young, soft, slim, silky. Her bare feet touched the flagstones like musical notes; she moved fast because the flagstones were frying-pan hot. Oakley watched her settle down on a lawn chaise under a beach umbrella. The dark green bikini set off her pale red hair. She was a tall girl with good bones.

Oakley had watched her grow up. Through her teens she had left a wake of dazed prep-school boys stunned by grieving, frustrated desire. There had been a serious boy friend a year or so ago but that had broken up, suddenly and unaccountably. It had happened not long before Earle Jr. had died.

Oakley recalled that time with unhappy vividness. Louise had called him at midnight tearfully to plead with him to fly down immediately: they had just received word of the boy's death and Conniston was falling apart. Oakley had held Conniston's hand for almost a week. He had lied steadfastly in a grim attempt to convince Conniston the boy's death wasn't his fault. In fact if anybody was to blame it was Conniston. Earle Jr. had strangled himself at a pot party with a girl's stocking.

Not amazing, in the cold glare of statistics: suicide was the second most common cause of death among college students in the United States. The boy's father, now barking heartily on the telephone, had never finished college—the football injury in his sophomore year had killed his scholarship. Thirty-seven years later Conniston had done what so many of them did: expected too much of his son, put too much pressure on him. Earle Jr. had never had time to relax and find himself. He'd been railroaded through prep academies and an ivy university and he'd killed himself, one year ago last month.

He was aware, suddenly, that Conniston was no longer talking; Conniston was standing at his elbow.

"Sorry," Oakley said. "Reveries, I guess. How are you, Earle?"

"Fine, fine. I keep fit." Conniston even took moralistic credit for his health; it was like him. In fact, near sixty, he looked closer to forty, as robust and hearty as he had been a quarter-century ago. His eyes, the color of rusty iron, slid past Oakley—a casual trick to mask his quick but careful scrutiny. The eyes traveled on by to give the sky half a second's uninterested inspection: "Beautiful day."

"Uh-huh. I wasn't looking at the weather." Oakley smiled around his unlit cigar.

"Terry? Stunning."

"Dazzling enough to make me wish I was twenty years younger."

"Might not matter," Conniston said. "She's ripe for somebody's bait. Desperately looking for love and doesn't even know what it is. You want to try, I won't stand in your way. Snappish little bitch, though. That outfit she's wearing, not much more than a little titty rag and a diaper. Adams said when she bought it they wrapped it in the price tag."

"Adams who?"

"Frankie Adams. House guest—one of Louise's charities. You didn't bump into him? You will." Conniston's face, expressionless, revealed his opinion of the unseen Frankie Adams. He added abstractedly, "Comedian. Does imitations. Impressions, he calls them—does a pretty good Nixon."

Conniston went back to his chair, indicating the pleasantries were over; Oakley stirred, went around the desk and sat. Without preamble he said, "You've got a feeder herd of five thousand head close to proper weight and grade. They've got to go to market within the next three months. Beef prices are pretty volatile right now—God knows if you'll even cover costs."

"So?"

"So I think it's time to start rounding them up."

"It's only August, Carl."

"Right. You can get a jump on the market."

"And what if market goes up?"

"What if it goes down? You know I'm not a nervous Nellie but I don't like the smell of it. The stock market's been drifting down and I expect commodities to start leveling off pretty quick."

"Better put a few more pounds on them, take the gamble. '

"That could be a quarter-million-dollar gamble, Earle."

"Peanuts. I'll take risk. Anything else?"

"When you liquidated your big board fund you asked me to scout around for a capital investment. Have you still got that cash free?"

"Most of it. Come up with something?"

"Half a mile of beach front on St. Croix in the Virgin Islands. The developers are getting thirty thousand per half acre for choice spots on St. Thomas and the boom will hit St. Croix next —you might recall Will Rogers' advice, buy land because they're not making any more of it."

"Will Rogers wasn't a businessman. You scouted St. Croix?"

"Of course."

"All right. Buy it."

That was settled; not even a handshake was needed. Oakley smiled briefly. "That's all at my end." He clamped his jaws on a cigar and sat back, ready to learn why Conniston had summoned him today.

Conniston's eyelids drooped, covering his thoughts. The reddish eyelashes were so pale they seemed hairless. "You talk to Louise?"

"A little. Storm signals are up, it appears."

"She tell you her pet project of month?"

"No. She only complained about feeling neglected and abandoned."

"Trying to teach her a lesson," Conniston said. The delivery —as if he were dictating a telegram—was the same as usual; the tone was gruffer than ordinary. "Orozco got her ear," he said.

"Oh-oh. And she bought it?"

"God save us from eastern liberal women without brains. She bought it."

"What do you want me to do about it?"

"Talk to Orozco. Your friend, not mine—won't listen to me."

Oakley said uncertainly, "Orozco's a damned good snoop, the best in the state. I'd hate to lose him."

"Private detectives are dime-a-dozen. Rather lose him than have him on my back all the time. Now he's put the bug in my wife's ear—I hear it all day long. Carl, you've got to inform fat pest I won't have any more of it."

Oakley couldn't help smiling—that a fat Mexican private detective and a 120-pound woman could cause Earle Conniston such discomfiture was absurd and comical.

Oakley said, "On the face of it Orozco's people have a real grievance."

"Then let them take it up with courts and OEO and civil rights people. Carl, I've given up on it. I can't seem to get it into heads of these silly *chicanos* that I own this place. Damn *chicanos* just can't adjust to the times. Fantastic land-grant pipe-dream can't change fact that I'm in possession with clean, clear title to land."

"They don't see it that way. The Mexicans claim this land is theirs by bequest from Ferdinand and Isabella."

Conniston snorted.

Oakley said, "The viceroys of New Spain deeded the Tierra Roja land grant to the Spanish settlers. After the Mexican War the Treaty of Guadalupe Hidalgo in 1848 guaranteed the American government would protect the property rights of Mexican landowners with legitimate deeds. Now the *chicanos* claim the gringos came in and destroyed the old Spanish documents in the Mexican archives and got the *chicanos'* land claims struck down by fraud in rigged Anglo courts."

"Not bad. You memorize that for delivery on TV or what? You working for the *chicanos* now, Carl?"

"No. But I've listened to them and looked up some law. The *chicanos* have got a pretty persuasive case."

"Aagh," Conniston said in disgust. "Those Spanish charters—scraps of paper signed in Madrid three hundred years ago.

Worthless. Those and a few guns took land away from Indians. So what? Tell *chicanos* to go argue with Papago Indians, not with me. I've got possession. Nine tenths of law, right?"

"Nothing's that simple any more. Look at the reparations the Alaska tribes got from the government."

"Then tell the *chicanos* go argue with government. Look, Carl, I don't want big federal case here. All I want is to get Diego Orozco off my wife's back so my wife will get off mine. Read me?"

Without waiting an answer Conniston got up and turned his back to scowl out through the window. Oakley brooded at his wide back. It looked taut, as if awaiting an expected stabbing. Conniston was too agitated; now, thinking back over the past year, Oakley recalled things—little things—which he had put out of his mind at the time because they had seemed inconsequential. Added together they began to form a disquieting picture. *I should have seen it before.* Conniston had started his fitful, furtive retreat when his son had killed himself; ever since, the overreactions had become more and more frequent, almost paranoid. Conniston was on the downhill slope—things had begun to go by too fast for him. Once, in June, he had disclosed dark suspicions that someone was trying to wrest his empire from him by secret maneuver—vague remarks about corporate raiders, fears of proxy fights. He had recovered the next day— "Forget that, forget that; I get moods sometimes, never mind" —but now Oakley recalled the incident and his mind jumped the straight track of all the years of conditioned thinking.

Watching the big man's back, the shoulders lifted defensively, Oakley said in a soft voice from which he withdrew all honest feeling, "I'll talk to Orozco, Earle. I'll take care of it."

He didn't notice Conniston's reply. A new and terrifying ambition had crept into Oakley's mind like an infiltrating cloud.

CHAPTER **Five**

The girl whom newspapers relentlessly identified as "Industrial Heiress Terry Conniston," disregarding the fact her father was still very much alive, emerged like a glossy mermaid from the blue pool, her chestnut hair wet-dark and shining in the sun. She slipped graceful feet into rubber thong-sandals and walked with a trim display of shapely thighs and swelling calves toward the veranda door of her bedroom, a tall girl with a good long-waisted carriage and the trim long legs of her western generation. The delicate lines and high strong cheekbones of her face seemed a denial of her father's blunt-boned genes.

In the shade by her door she stopped to look back across the painfully glistening pool. Patches of benign clouds rode quickly across the sky from the west, dragging their shadows along the ground, and for a moment she enjoyed watching the afternoon colors change on the grass hills. Occasional dots on the slopes were her father's cattle grazing; once she saw the dust of a running jeep on the skyline. Her face turned youthfully solemn and she brooded toward the pool, squinting; she was blue-eyed but she detested sunglasses and never wore them. She was remembering the starry evening two years ago when she had returned home from her first semester at Bennington to find the enormous pool, newly built—"A little surprise I had put in for you," her father had said, putting his thick arm across her shoulders and walking her along the flagstones. Half a dozen muscular young men with golden tans had been splashing in the pool and Terry had remarked, "I see you've stocked it for me, Daddy," and they had laughed. Those had been happier times.

She detected movement in the corner of her vision and shifted her glance to see the stirring of a screen door at the end of the far wing of the house. She had a glimpse of Frankie Adams' lizard-narrow shape before the comedian disappeared inside. Irritated, she wondered how long he had been standing there watching her. He was a creepy one—one of Louise's friends from show business. He had a worn-out slimy quality like old clothes with too much shine on them. She couldn't understand why her father tolerated Adams; but then she hadn't understood her father for a long time anyway.

She went inside, showered, dried her hair, put on a gray Neiman-Marcus minidress and matching sandals and looked at herself critically in the mirror. *The female Dorian Grey,* she thought. Glow of tan over fair young skin; a face somehow innocent of the fury raging inside.

Hair tumbling loose over one shoulder, handbag and schoolbooks clutched in her arm, she hurried out of her room into the corridor; she intended to go right by the office but her father came out—as if he had been lying in wait—and blocked her way. "Hi. Being exclusive, Baby?"

I wish you wouldn't call me that. "Hi." Her smile was quick and false. Behind him she saw Carl Oakley in the office, tall and good-looking, preoccupied; Oakley mirrored her uncomfortable smile. Business problems, she guessed—they both looked wrung-out. *Whatever it is, I'm sure money will fix it. Money always does.* Her father's answer to her every problem was, *Here—buy yourself a pretty thing.*

Her father frowned earnestly. "Leaving early?"

"Something I want to look up in the university library before class." It was a lie: she had to get out of this house.

"Uh," he said, too indifferent to press her. He made a half-turn back into the office but then he changed his mind, stopped, watched her. "We ought to make time to talk. Hell of a busy summer somehow, time just frittering away."

Don't tell me about all the things you haven't had time for.

I'm at the top of the list. She glanced at Carl Oakley. Now might be a good time, with Carl standing there—Carl would be a brake on her father. She said, "Summer term ends next week, you know. After exams I think I'll go to New York." She had a smoky voice.

He was shocked. "New York? What about Bennington? What about school?"

"I'm sick of it—I need a break. I'll take a semester off, what's wrong with that? Maybe I'll go back in the spring."

"But——" He looked around over his shoulder, seeking help from Oakley, who only looked on judiciously and said nothing. "What can you do in New York? Buy better clothes? Drink better wine? It's just as good right here."

She halved her nervous smile. "I guess I just want to try it on for size," she said, and stepped past him.

"Wait."

She made a half-turn and looked at him slantwise, her hair swinging forward across her face. Her father spread his hands helplessly. "Can't talk to you. Why can't we talk to each other any more?"

"Let's skip it, Daddy."

"No. Been skipping it too long. Christ, all our children deserve better parents. You can't live very long without hurting someone, Baby—I've made my mistakes. But don't just run out on me without a word."

It was so unlike him to feel at fault that she only stared. Where had all this sudden guilt come from? She hadn't said a word! Past him, moving forward to fill the office doorway with his wide shoulders, Carl Oakley wore a worried frown which he wiped off his face quickly when Conniston turned a beseeching glance toward him. She noticed in her father's cheek a rhythmic tic she had never seen before. Her father said, "Maybe you're right—maybe you need a break. You've been in school what, fifteen years, fourteen? Suppose you take a few months off, go to Europe. Maybe you and Louise could go together"—Terry made a face but he didn't see it—"buy some clothes, bring back some paintings, go skiing in Austria Christmastime. How'd that be? I'll arrange all the tickets."

Had he never realized his kind of checkbook generosity killed love? "Daddy, please, for heaven's sake!" *What do you want now? You've never missed me. You've never shared anything with me.*

His shoulders lifted. "If you're a single girl in New York—look, the place is just no good for you."

She said wearily, "Please stop treating me like a child."

"Why should I? You're a star-spangled adolescent, Baby."

"With a mind of her own," she shot back, and wheeled away.

He caught her by the elbow and spun her around; she almost lost her balance. His fist hurt her arm; she winced and he withdrew it quickly, but not before a sudden hot rage flooded the tissues of her body with a debilitating shortness of breath. "Let go of me—leave me alone!" She took a step backward and braced a hand against the corridor wall.

A dark scowl clouded his face. "Look at her, Carl. What about this escapist generation? Get tired of college so they just bug out —got the attention span of a six-year-old. Baby, time you learned to finish what you start."

"You were ready ten seconds ago to send me to Europe on a spree."

"A chance most girls would give their eyeteeth for. You turned it down—why? Out of spite. What have I done to make you hate me?"

Back to that again. She couldn't make him out; he frightened her—and, by frightening her, angered her beyond reason.

He dragged the back of a hand across his mouth. "Baby——"

"Don't call me that!" Her voice had climbed; she clamped her lips shut and backed away. Oakley came out of the doorway and put a hand on her father's arm. Her father shook his head as if dazed and Terry spun toward the front of the house, almost running. She batted through the front room, ignoring Louise's startled question; ran to the carport and climbed into the red Fiberglas Daimler sports car, tossing books and handbag onto the seat and turning the key hard enough to bend it. When the engine caught she backed out with a spray of gravel and manhandled the car viciously toward the gate. By the time she passed the feeder corrals the Daimler's eight cylinders were

roaring; she fishtailed onto the graded main road at forty miles an hour and kept the pedal floored until the little red car was doing eighty and a speck of thrown dust in her eye brought her back to reality. She rubbed her eye and let the car coast down to a reasonable speed, feeling tear-moisture against her finger. She was sure now that there was no meeting ground with him. She didn't understand him and never would; he was beyond understanding. The only way to get along with him would be at a distance, where they might achieve some precarious truce; but close to him, she hated him. *I do hate him—he's right. God, I hate him.* He had killed her brother. He had driven her mother away, first to the concert stage, then to the sanitarium where she languished now in alcohol-corroded unreality. *He'll do something to me too if I don't get away.*

The wind caught the cover of a book on the passenger seat and flipped it open. She slapped it shut and turned it around on the seat with its spine to the wind. *Modern Literary Criticism.* The classroom would calm her down. It was a calm place, isolated, locked away from the rest of the world—a place where *P.R.* meant not public relations but *Partisan Review.* A room full of pot-smoking short-haired girls and long-haired boys with shaggy moustaches. It was a world that would never be hers, any more than her father's would be; she despised his world of wealth and business but she would never fit into a literary ivory tower. By the cruel trick of birth she had been forced into a circumstance where the simple desire to be a woman—unsophisticated, without intellectual or financial pretense, just a *woman* to make a home and have babies—was denied her.

Seething, her mind on fire, not knowing what she wanted or how she felt, she drove at four thirty past a dusty side road that led to some forgotten destination across the hills; a dusty car was parked along the shoulder with two or three vague shapes inside but she didn't notice it when she went by at sixty miles an hour. Four hours from now she would return by this route and pass the same side road.

Dressed casually for dinner, Oakley entered the splendid dark-oak dining room shortly after six o'clock in time to see

Earle Conniston pour a glass of gin and anoint it with a few drops of vermouth. Conniston had got a grip on himself after Terry's stormy departure and hadn't said a word about it since. Oakley, his eyes narrowed with conjecture, was only faintly aware of Louise's approach until she snapped her fingers in front of him and laughed gaily—too gaily, he thought—and, having gained his attention, presented him to the house guest, Frankie Adams, who wore Bermuda shorts and a loud short-sleeved Hawaiian sports shirt, garments which revealed undue lengths of unattractive bony legs and flaccid hairy arms. Adams had a small round head dominated by the biggest nose Oakley had ever seen.

Shaking the little man's hand was like gripping a fresh-caught trout. Making conversation, Oakley said, "That's a pretty wild shirt."

"Yeah. It got arrested twice." Frankie Adams grinned, showing capped teeth. His hair was slicked back, thick and Indian-black; his narrow face was meticulously shaved to minimize a Mediterranean beard-stubble and he smelled of expensive after-shave. He had the knowing eye of an accomplished procurer, the raspy voice of a pitchman; whatever his past, it had burdened him with a stealthy appearance; yet for all that, Oakley did not find him disagreeable. (He recalled a remark of Conniston's an hour ago, sour reference to Adams: "Been here six days now. No telling when we'll get rid of him. Some people can stay longer in a week than others can in a year.")

Oakley said desultorily, "You and Louise knew each other in New York."

"Worked some of the same teevee shows," Adams said, and struck an Ed Sullivan pose. "And on our shew t'night, lez an' gennulmen, the wunnenonly LLLOOOOZE HARRIS, straight from her starrn role on Browway with Misser HENNRY FONNA—Now lessere it for Franchie Athams, lez an' gennulmen, Franchie Athams!"

Adams bowed to the audience and coughed behind his wrist.

Conniston came from the side bar with a small round wooden tray holding four drinks. It did not escape Oakley that the liquid in the drinks trembled. Louise was still laughing merrily at

Adams' imitation of Sullivan; Oakley had to admit it had been uncanny, even considering Sullivan's imitability. The tone and quality of the voice had been exact, the phrasing perfect. Adams wheeled toward Louise and launched into Henry Fonda doing a Wyatt Earp speech from *My Darling Clementine,* which convulsed her; Conniston looked on, unamused. Louise's tawny hair gathered light; unconsciously she struck theatrical poses in Adams' company. ("Seems the sonofabitch out of work," Conniston had explained. "Camping out with old buddies until his agent can get him bookings. Says he's broke because he played slow horses. Told me his father was always ahead of his time, went bankrupt in 1928, which was supposed to break me up in helpless laughter. Can't stand the debauched little bastard." Understandable, now that Oakley had met Adams: the comedian had a flip manner of a sort offensive to the sanctimonious—and Conniston, in his profane way, was the most pious of men.)

Conniston stood a slight distance apart, drinking quickly, watching Adams distastefully. Suddenly Adams turned toward Oakley, breaking off his drawl, and winked brashly. "Tell you what, Carl, send message Cairo cancel Russian oil leases or we pull out. Hell with widows and orphans. What's one lousy billion? Teach sonabitch Arabs thing or two. Make him realize Conniston important man."

Adams was halfway through the speech before any of them caught on to the fact that he was doing Conniston—and doing him with eerie accuracy, down to the shoulderlifting gesture and the fast blink of eyes. The speech completed, Adams settled back to await applause. It was forthcoming only from Louise. Embarrassed, Oakley did not stir. Conniston drew himself up. Adams beamed at him, dapper and pouter-pigeon-proud. "You ready for that, hey?"

"I don't find that amusing," Conniston remarked. He turned his back to Adams and strode across the room to the bar.

Adams' face fell; Louise said, "Really, darling"—calling her husband "darling" with steely emphasis.

Conniston mixed a fresh martini for himself before he replied; then, turning to face them, he said caustically, "Don't tell me you're afraid I've put guest's nose out of joint."

Trying to cut the tension, Adams said weakly, "Let's have no loose remarks about my nose." He tried to smile. With a nervous gesture toward his feet he said, "I sure admire your house, Earle. Never saw a carpet like this—you need snowshoes to travel it. Oh hell, never mind me, I thought it was funny, hey? Didn't mean to insult you. Chalk it up I've spent too many years in fourth-rate clubs MC'ing blue acts. MC, that's Mental Case, hey? Look, I'm sorry, okay?"

Oakley watched the jewel-hard shine of Louise's glance against Conniston. Conniston shook his head and threw back his head to drain the martini at one gulp; afterward he said, "All right—all right. Didn't mean to fly off handle. Been a lousy day —apologize."

"Sure—sure," Adams said, and stood silent, having run out of things to say.

"Really!" Louise breathed, and strode toward the kitchen, walking with a magnificent jounce and heave of young buttocks which seemed to writhe with a life of their own. Oakley caught the way Adams stared at her, unblinking. He distinctly heard Adams whisper, "Yes sirree Bob," although it was plain Conniston didn't catch it. When Oakley threw a direct glance at Adams the comedian met it with a guileless lecherous wink. Oakley turned half away and closed his eyes. So that was how it was: Louise's childish revenge. She would use Adams to pay Conniston back for his "neglect." That was why she had uttered her extraordinary plea earlier: "He just shuts me out. What can I do?" She had been absolving herself of the blame for it. Trying to convince Oakley that whatever happened was Earle's fault, not hers. She was an actress; she needed an audience to applaud her performance; she wanted Oakley's good opinion.

She must hate Earle terribly to do it right here in his own house under his nose. Watching Conniston's broad tense back as Conniston poured himself a third drink, Oakley thought, *I don't know if I can blame her.*

A few hours later the phone rang.

CHAPTER Six

Mitch Baird squatted brooding on his haunches. Below him he could see the road winding north through the hills. The heat, rising from the earth in the dusk, sucked sweat from his pores. Out across the flayed surrealist landscape dust-devils funneled erratically in yellow wheelings of sand and twigs and leaves.

He turned around on his heels. Floyd Rymer nodded and smiled. Beyond Floyd, down in the dry arroyo, Mitch could see the dusty Oldsmobile. Theodore and Billie Jean were in the back seat. Georgie Rymer sat on a rock near the car, yawning and scratching.

Floyd looked at his watch. "Another forty minutes, about."

Mitch's eyes flickered when they touched Floyd's. Floyd said, "Your mouth looks like a coathanger. Smile. You're about to break out in dollar signs, remember?"

Mitch drew in a deep breath. "I don't like this. It's too risky."

"Nothing's risky if the stakes are high enough. Mitch, methinks you complain too much." The hooded gray eyes smiled lazily with cool disdain.

"They'll be after us for stealing that Olds, you know."

"Relax. These country cops have trouble finding the chief of police. The license plates are clean."

Mitch held his tongue. No point arguing with Floyd. All he wanted was to get away from the whole nightmare. But Floyd hadn't let him out of his sight.

Floyd's eyes, wary and predatory, scrutinized him with secret amusement. "You know what you're supposed to do."

"Yeah—yeah." Mitch felt sick. "But the whole thing's stupid."

"On the contrary. Mitch?"

"What?"

"You fuck this one up and I'll feed you to the birds. Understood?" Floyd took the snub-barrel revolver out of his windbreaker pocket and spun it casually on his finger like a gunslinger in a Western movie. It was the only gun in the group. Floyd didn't trust anyone else with one.

"Take heart, Mitch," Floyd breathed. "Into each life a little loot must fall." He smiled and got to his feet like a cobra uncoiling. *"Après vous, mon ami."* He gestured with the .38, still smiling.

Mitch got to his feet and climbed carefully down to the car. His desert-boots dislodged pebbles and made a tiny avalanche that spilled into the arroyo with a racket. Forewarned by the noise, Billie Jean opened the back door of the car and adjusted her dress down around her meaty hips while she climbed out. Theodore made a lunge for her, missed, and barked an obscenity; he came roaring out of the car and got the laughing girl in a hammerlock.

Floyd came off the hill and stood with his feet braced, scowling. "All right, get untangled, you two. *Georgie?*"

Georgie appeared beyond the car, coming forward, trying to walk like his brother. "Everything okay?"

Floyd looked at his watch. "Seven o'clock, and all's well."

"I could use a jolt," Georgie complained. "You know. A cat gets tense, time like this?"

"You'll get one," Floyd said. Theodore and Billie Jean stirred, came forward toward the hood of the car and ranged themselves alongside Georgie. Mitch hung back. Floyd gave him a dry glance and said, "What ho. Everybody ready?"

"Hail, hail," Mitch muttered dryly, "the gang's all here." Floyd's irrelevant humor was contagious. He realized that and made a face.

He caught Floyd's caustic grin; Floyd said, "All right, Mitch, cool the wit. Get the flashlight, that's a good boy."

Mitch went past the others to the car and got the flashlight out of the glove compartment. He tested it twice and put it in his hip pocket. Floyd made some nonvocal signal behind his back; by the time he turned, he saw Theodore opening the trunk of the car. Theodore removed various pieces of wood and began to assemble a pair of sawhorses. Floyd said, "Lend a hand, Mitch."

Mitch helped Theodore carry the sawhorses and detour signs and firepot bombs to the edge of the main road. When he looked back he could see Floyd watching him, one hand in the pocket that contained the revolver. Floyd's expression was unreadable in the dimming twilight. He heard Floyd talking out of the side of his mouth to Billie Jean:

"Remember what to look for. Little red sports car with a girl driving. You'll see it come under the bright lights at the freeway ramp when she gets off."

Billie Jean said, "I just flash at you, right?"

"That's all, sweetness. But you had better be God damn sure it's the right car."

Mitch's lips pinched together; for a moment he felt faint. He knew what to expect before he heard Floyd speak: "Mitch, come over here and give the flashlight to Billie Jean."

Mitch swallowed an oath and came forward, Theodore tramping heavily behind him. He gave the light to the girl. She swayed her bottom at Theodore. "Rub it for luck."

When the girl had climbed the hill to her lookout post and Theodore had gone back to the road, Floyd said to Mitch, "You didn't really think I was going to let you go up there by yourself, did you?"

Keeping a neutral tone by an effort of will, Mitch said, "I thought you might. I've seen the car before. Billie Jean hasn't. What if she makes a mistake?"

"She won't. Part of my genius, old cock, is that I never expect people to do more than they're capable of doing. Billie Jean has the best eyesight of anybody in this bunch. And she's not as likely to take a powder over the far side of the hill as some people I might mention."

"If you're so sure I'm not going to be any help why keep me here?"

"I've got a use for you, old cock. Don't worry about it."

Georgie was standing hip-shot against the front fender of the car, rubbing his nose. His eyes were red, his movements taut. His eyes looked dull and indifferent; he said in a complaining whine, "Hey, Floyd?"

"Okay, okay." Irritated, Floyd went over to the car. Georgie was watching him unblinkingly. Floyd got into the car and said, "Mitch, come over here where I can see you. Georgie, turn around."

Mitch walked forward reluctantly. A slow anticipatory smile spread across Georgie's gray face and he turned around to face away from the car, folded his arms as smugly as a child awaiting a surprise birthday present, and closed his eyes.

Floyd fumbled inside the car for a minute before he opened the door and got out holding a syringe that glistened dully in the failing light. He struck a match and held the needle in the flame, saying tonelessly, "We wouldn't want the kid to catch hepatitis from a dirty needle, would we?" Afterward he turned his smiling brother around like a mannequin and plunged the needle into the vein in the crook of Georgie's elbow. Georgie was tense; now he threw his head back and grinned, his mouth sagging open in slow ecstasy.

Floyd dropped the plastic syringe and crushed it under his heel. There were plenty more where it had come from. He said gently, "Get in the car, Georgie," and helped his brother into the back seat. Georgie slumped back with his eyes shut, rolling his face from side to side, moaning softly. Floyd shut the door on him and stood for a moment frowning at the ground. Then he stirred. "Come on."

Mitch followed him over to the road. Theodore was sitting on one of the sawhorses, dangling one leg; Theodore's grotesquely scarred face was ghoulish in the falling darkness. Floyd said mildly, "We all know what to do. Watch the hill for Billie Jean's signal. Theodore, if Mitch here gets cold feet you can warm them up for him."

Theodore said, "Yeah."

"Meanwhile stick your finger back in your nose."

Mitch kept wary watch on Theodore—the gleam of his one good eye, the heavy roll of his brutal lips. Theodore would enjoy a chance to knock him around. Bleakly Mitch turned his back and stared at the hilltop. He could barely make out Billie Jean's plump silhouette against the night sky.

The signal light flashed.

"All right," Floyd murmured. "Move."

They lit the firepots and set them out in the road, blocking off the passage with the sawhorses. Detour with arrows pointing to the right into the narrow dusty side road that led nowhere. Fifty yards up the arroyo the Oldsmobile stood across the side road, making it a cul-de-sac.

Theodore touched Mitch on the shoulder and Mitch unhappily followed him across the road into the brush, where he crouched down with Theodore's hand on his shoulder, keeping him captive. He could hear the rattle of dislodged stones as Billie Jean hurried down the hill to join Floyd by the Olds.

Headlights came over a rise and stabbed the night, throwing their harsh brightness against the sawhorses, and he heard the snarl of the engine, the change in its tone when the driver discovered the obstacle and down-shifted. There was a brief squeal of rubber—she had been traveling fast. The little sports car came into sight, darkly red in its own reflected lamplight, slowed to a crawl, the girl plainly visible and frowning with baffled irritation, and turned off into the cul-de-sac, bumping along on its butt-jolting springs. The headlights picked up the Olds and the brake-lights flashed brightly. The sports car slowed to a halt, the girl's head lifting alertly. Floyd's leonine shape leaped from the shadows to her right. He jumped into the car with both feet, lighting on the right-hand bucket seat, and crouched forward to twist the keys and yank them out of the ignition before the girl had time to react. The rumble of the engine died with a chatter and dust swirled in the headlights.

Theodore said in his ear, "Okay, okay. Let's go." Theodore dragged him onto the road and they picked up the sawhorses and firepots and carried them into the cul-de-sac. Mitch heard the brief sound of a struggle, a girl's high shriek cut off in its middle; he couldn't see through the dust. The headlights were switched off; he stumbled and almost dropped his armload. "Go on," Theodore said testily behind him. "Pick up your feet."

"I can't see in the dark," Mitch snapped.

Someone turned on the headlights again. Billie Jean was bent over the passenger door of the sports car, tying a gag in the captive girl's mouth. Floyd climbed out of the car and grinned, his face flushed with excitement. "She's a great little fighter for her weight."

Mitch carried the sawhorses back to the trunk of the Olds and put them inside. Theodore extinguished the firepots, put everything away in the trunk and slammed the lid. They walked back to the sports car. Floyd and Billie Jean had the girl outside, on her feet. Her hands were tied together in front of her with coat-hanger wire. Spirited and beautiful, she held Floyd with a surly glance of steel contempt. If she was afraid she concealed it well. She was disheveled and scratched up; Mitch thought, *She's gorgeous,* and sucked in his breath.

When he came closer he saw the telltale thread of moisture on her upper lip. Scared but game. Floyd came around the car and chucked the girl under the chin. "Delicious, isn't she? A hundred and twenty pounds of pure platinum. How about it now, Mitch? Piece of cake."

When Theodore looked at the girl his neck swelled with musty desire. Theodore said, "How about we all knock off a piece before we go?"

The girl blanched; her eyes flashed toward Floyd. Floyd said to her, "Don't be too offended. Theodore has an unfortunate manner. He's a wonderful example of the miracle by which a human body can function without the help of mental power." He wheeled: "Keep your hands and your mouth off her, Theodore. The lady's our guest."

Theodore worked up saliva in his mouth and spat emphatically on the ground. Turning away, he said, "She looks cold tittie anyway." Billie Jean glared at him.

Floyd said mildly, "Put her in the Olds. Theodore, you'll drive her car. Let's go."

The two cars prowled quickly across the graded desert roads, twisting through the hills. They turned north once and ran five miles along an unpaved secondary road, mainly because Floyd wanted to throw pursuit off in case the police had instruments capable of identifying their tire tracks. They turned west on a paved highway and south again after another five-mile run, going down a gravel road toward the Mexican border. Fifteen miles short of that boundary Floyd indicated a turn to the left and Mitch put the Olds into a narrow pair of rocky ruts that took them uncomfortably, even at five miles an hour, through a notch in the hills. Beyond the notch the country leveled out and the road surface became slightly smoother although it was evident the road was seldom used or graded. Once they passed a weathered sign: DIP—WARNING—QUICKSAND—DO NOT ENTER WHEN WET.

The moon came up; Floyd said, "We're just about there. Take it easy along here."

"What do you think I'm doing? I wish to hell somebody'd taught Theodore not to tailgate so close."

"Good brakes in those little cars," Floyd observed. "He can stop on a dime. Don't worry about it."

"What if the dime happens to be in my pocket?"

"Very droll."

In the back seat the girl after trying to talk through the gag in her mouth had subsided. Billie Jean sat watching her maliciously.

Mitch said, "What's her name again?"

"Terry Conniston," Floyd said. He held up the girl's handbag. "I checked, to make sure. We got the right girl."

"Be funny if we hadn't."

"How kind of you to remind me." Floyd hipped around in the seat. "Beautiful girl, isn't she, Mitch?"

"Why ask me?"

"I thought you were taken with her."

"What are you driving at now?"

Floyd only chuckled.

"Endsville," muttered Billie Jean. The dark little desert town had a cemetery look. After the maze of signless dirt roads Mitch was surprised Floyd had found it on the first try. It was a sprawl of melting adobe relics, half concealed by clumped cactus and mesquite—a ramshackle disarray in various states of caved-in collapse. Empty windows stared dark and vacant from a few shells left standing.

They drove into a barn. It was pitch-black when they turned off the lights. Floyd took the flashlight and said, "Everybody out," and stood by the car holding the beam toward the wide front door to light their path. Mitch waited for Billie Jean to push the prisoner out of the car; Terry Conniston's knees buckled and Mitch reached out to catch her. He heard Billie Jean snicker when he picked up the girl and half-carried her outside.

They stumbled over debris, across the ghost street. The faded lettering crescent-shaped across the high front of the building was hardly readable when the flashlight played across it, General Mercantile. The sign on the door said the store was closed. It had been drawn freehand, red paint on wood. An old metal RC Cola sign creaked and banged in the rusty breeze. Billie Jean looked around and said again, "Endsville. Pillsville. Christ. I'm hungry and dusty and I don't s'pose there's anyplace to take a bath around here."

Georgie stood off in the background, blinking drowsily, just coming around from his jolt of horse. Mitch felt the captive girl's warm weight against him. She had gone limp but she hadn't fainted; forcing them to carry her was her form of protest.

Floyd went in with the light, ducking under a fallen beam. "Bring her in here." The musty place had been stripped of interior appointments. Strips of faded wallpaper hung from the walls; the windows had rags stuffed in them; most of the room was a foot deep in rubble. The flashlight beam stabbed one corner: "Set her down over there."

Mitch lowered her very gently, eliciting Billie Jean's cackle: "She won't break, Mitch."

The light went out. In the absolute blackness Mitch heard the girl catch her breath and then Floyd struck a match and touched it to the wick of a blackened oil lamp with an old-fashioned chimney. The weak yellow light flickered up into cobwebbed corners. Mitch sneezed and stayed where he was, on one knee on the floor beside Terry Conniston. She sat with her back against the wall, arms wrapped around her knees, glaring at all of them with icy scorn. She looked fragile and slim, young, virginal.

Floyd said, "Everybody pay attention. Nobody opens the door again unless we put the light out first, understand? You can spot a light from forty miles away out here. All right Mitch, take the gag off her."

Mitch reached around warily, watching the girl's eyes. Billie Jean edged close and said, "She looks kind of sad."

"That's all right," said Theodore, "I'm the comforting type." He gave a hooting bray of laughter that rang back from the roofbeams.

"Take it easy," Mitch murmured, clumsy with the knot at the back of her head. The girl uttered short nervous little gasps every time he touched her. Her eyes were narrowed, sullen, trying to hold back fear. When he removed the scarf she spat out the wadded handkerchief and licked her lips fiercely.

Floyd came over with his knapsack and sat down crosslegged like an Indian, smiling amiably. He took the small tape-recorder out and connected various plugs and pushed buttons, and said, "One, two, three, four, five," into the microphone, then played it back for a test and ran the tape back to the beginning. Terry Conniston watched, not speaking, rigid with uncertainty and fear. Above them, one shoulder propped against the wall, Theodore opened the snap-ring top of a beer can with a pop and a hiss. In the unsteady yellow light his face was a violent mask of raw evil.

Floyd said, "Miss Conniston, please pay attention."

The girl stared. Her eyes whipped toward Floyd. Mitch leaned past her legs and lifted the canteen out of the knapsack, unscrewed the top and offered it to her. Terry Conniston shook her head, not removing her eyes from Floyd, who spoke to her in a gentle voice:

"I guess you've figured out what we're up to. You're being held for ransom. We'll be getting in touch with your father and making arrangements and when the ransom's paid you'll be turned loose. Nobody's going to hurt you. You understand?"

She nodded cautiously, her long eyes wide open. It occurred to Mitch she was afraid to speak. He reached out to touch her hand reassuringly but she drew it away.

Floyd said, "Now, if you agree not to give us any trouble we'll take the wire off your wrists. You'd like that, wouldn't you?"

The girl made no reply of any kind. Floyd said patiently, "Look, honey, this won't do. You see this tape-recorder? You're going to talk into it for me."

Mute and stubborn, she shook her head. When she looked down at the recorder her hair swung forward, masking her face. She pushed her lower lip forward to blow hair off her forehead. She was stunning, Mitch thought.

Floyd closed his eyes and seemed to be deep in thought. That was when Theodore spoke up: "Hell, let me do it. I can make her talk."

Floyd threw his head back. "Theodore, this discussion does not include you. Butt out. When you want to talk to me you raise your hand." His eyes burned against Theodore until Theodore stirred in discomfort and drifted away, sucking beer.

Floyd turned back to the girl. He smiled. "Sweetness, don't make it rough on yourself. The longer you stall around, the longer it'll take to finish this. All you have to do is talk into the tape-recorder, tell the truth. We're not asking you to make up any lies."

Billie Jean said, "What if she tells where we are?"

"That's why they have erasing heads on tape-recorders," Floyd said, unruffled. "All right, Miss Conniston?"

Terry Conniston curled her lip. "Go crawl back under your rock."

Floyd's smile was thin. "Don't you want to be friendly, Sweetness? Then we'll put it this way. Either you rap with me or I turn Theodore loose on you. What do you say?"

Sulky silence was the girl's only answer until Floyd turned, making a show of regretful reluctance, and drew in a breath to call Theodore.

"Okay, damn you. Okay. What am I supposed to say?"

Floyd took the gun out of his pocket and held it casually, not

aimed at anything in particular. He handed the microphone to
Mitch and said, "I won't dictate anything. Use your own words.
Make it short because I'll be playing this back over the telephone and we don't want any long speeches that would give
your daddy time to put a tracer on the line. Just tell him you're
being held by people with guns and you want him to bail you
out. Tell him you're all right but we've threatened your life if
your daddy doesn't come across."

Floyd nodded to Mitch and pushed the button. The tape
began to whir softly. Mitch held the mike close to Terry Conniston's lips. She stared at it, frowned with concentration and
finally blinked at him. "I can't think of what to say."

Mitch opened his mouth but Floyd shook his head. The tape
hissed for at least a full minute before the girl closed her eyes
and said in a dull monotone, "Daddy, please listen. They're
recording this on tape. They've kidnaped me but I'm not hurt.
Please do what they want. . . . I can't think of anything else to
say. What else do you want me to say?"

Floyd switched the machine off. "That ought to be enough for
openers. Later he'll want confirmation and you'll have to talk
some more."

He ran the tape back and played it back, frowning; he listened to it twice before he shook his head and said, "It's no
good. Not enough feeling in your voice. You don't sound scared
enough."

"What do you want me to do? Tear my hair and shriek?"

Floyd smiled. "You're a cool one, Sweetness. It wouldn't hurt
for you to get choked up a little and bust out crying. Might
persuade your daddy to come through fast. Let's try it again."

Altogether they made four tapes; the last one satisfied Floyd.
By this time Terry Conniston was strained and weak with
nerves—qualities that came through on the tape. While Floyd
rewound the tape and packed the recorder in its leather case
she sat with her head back against the wall, eyes half closed,
breathing in flutters. Mitch gently unwound the wire from her
wrists. It hadn't cut her but the flesh was ugly with trenches and
ridges.

Theodore came over, crushing the empty beer can in one

hand; he said caustically, "You all done now?"

"For the moment."

"Okay. What do we do with her?"

"Well now," Floyd asked, "what do you suggest?"

"Bang her," Theodore replied immediately. "We all knock off a piece and then we bury her out here someplace."

Mitch heard the girl's quick indrawn breath. He looked up in a rage. "What's the matter with you? You got your brains up your ass or what?"

Theodore said, "What'd I say?"

Floyd muttered, "Miss Conniston, I apologize for our—colleague. Theodore is an unfortunate master of the subtle innuendo."

Theodore said, "What?"

"Mitch, explain it to Theodore. Wipe that vacant bewildered look off his face."

Angry, Mitch said without turning his head, "Explain it yourself."

Theodore said, "I don't get it. Look, we've got to kill her. She knows what we look like. It don't have to look like murder. Hell, take one of Georgie's needles, inject a little air-bubble into her vein. Fast and painless and no traces. What the hell?"

Terry Conniston watched him with terrified fascination. Floyd said, "You're beginning to exhaust my patience, Theodore. See if you can follow this. If we're going to get money for her we'll have to give them proof she's alive. They won't pay for a corpse."

"They ain't to know she's dead."

"They'll get the idea fast enough if we don't let her talk to them."

Over in the corner, yawning, Georgie patted his lips and smiled vacantly at the ceiling. Mitch envied him his obliviousness. Floyd said softly, "Not a finger, Theodore. You lay one finger on her and I'll have your hide in strips. Understand?"

"No," Theodore said. "No. I don't."

"Then let's just say I'm saving her for myself," Floyd said. "You understand that, don't you?"

"Whyn't you say so?"

"I just did." Floyd added in sotto voce disgust, "To be sure. Christ, I wish I could pay him what he's really worth. The minimum wage law wouldn't allow it." He got to his feet and caught Mitch's eye. "My fine buffoon, come over here a minute."

Mitch gave the girl a moment's solemn attention before he followed Floyd to the far corner of the old store, climbing over debris. The light was weak. Floyd stood loose, in an invertebrate attitude, looking somnolent with self-satisfaction. "I told you I had a use for you."

"Maybe I'm dense. You'll have to explain it to me."

"I'll lay it out in plain English. Pay attention. In a little while one of us has to leave here and get to the phone line, which is about fifteen miles north of here. Now if you take one look at our happy little family of mouth-breathers and nose-pickers you'll see there's only one of us who can be expected to say the right thing to Earle Conniston—only one of us who can make that phone call. Me. You agree?"

"What if I do?"

"While I'm gone somebody has to take charge here. Now, let's just suppose you decide to bug out as soon as I'm gone. What happens then? Can you make a guess?"

Mitch didn't have to guess. He knew. He nodded with a sour face. "Theodore will rape hell out of her and nobody'll stop him."

"He might and he might not. He knows he was right about one thing. If we turn her loose she can identify us. Theodore's not so stupid he can be talked out of the truth."

"Truth?"

"Booty is truth, truth booty. The moving finger hath writ, and it spelled five hundred thousand dollars. That's all you need to know, and all Theodore needs to know. In that little pea-sized brain of his he's matching up his share of it against the risk of being identified by the girl if we turn her loose alive."

"What's all this got to do with me?"

"When I leave to make the phone call, my fine idiot, you'll be the only thing standing between that girl and her death. I don't expect you to go over the hill. On the contrary. I expect you to stay here and protect our guest."

Mitch said slowly, "If she's going to be killed in the end anyway what difference does it make to me?"

"I thought you liked her."

"What gives you that idea?"

"The way you took charge. Come on, Mitch, you don't want her killed."

"I don't seem to have a whole lot of choice in it."

"You're wrong. I've got no intention of killing her."

"But you just said——"

"I was talking about Theodore, not me. Look at it from my point of view. If I can collect the money and remove myself from any possible apprehension what reason do I have to kill the girl?"

"That sounds great. Only how do you remove yourself from it if she's alive to identify you? Sooner or later they'll turn you up and extradite you."

"Not if I'm not me. Stop and think a minute, Mitch. The girl isn't the only one who can identify us."

"No?"

"It ought to be obvious that for each one of us there are at least four people who can identify us."

"Who?"

Floyd's glance flicked across the room, from face to face. He said softly, "We can all identify each other, Mitch."

"You should have thought of that before you started this thing."

"Ah, but I did. You don't think I'd be stupid enough to trust all of you? My junkie brother, those two brainless oafs, and you who want nothing more than to get away from this whole caper? Did you really think I hadn't taken that into account? You don't credit me with much sense, do you?"

"Nothing's making much sense right now."

"Then let me clear it up. There's a man in Mexico, a defrocked plastic surgeon who had the misfortune to be one of the perpetrators of Nazi human experiments during the war and hasn't been able to get a license to practice in any country. So he runs a little apothecary shop in a Mexican town where the Mafia has enough clout to keep the authorities off his back—he's done some favors for the Mafiosi. All it takes to purchase a new face and grafted fingerprint pads from him is a few thousand dollars. You understand now?"

Mitch had to absorb it. Finally he said, "It's groovy for you— what about the rest of us?"

"When we collect the ransom we'll split it five ways. That's the last you'll see of me. What happens after that is up to you. You and Theodore can fight over the girl."

"What about your brother?"

Floyd said with quiet heat, "He's an albatross around my neck. His share of the ransom will buy my freedom from him. Let him save himself or destroy himself with the money—it's his choice."

Floyd smiled slowly. Mitch remembered what he had said the other night: *Am I not a son of a bitch?* He stared across the dim room, past the guttering lamp at the sullen shape of the girl in the corner. Lamplight reflected frostily from the surfaces of her blue eyes. She was watching the two of them as if aware they were haggling over her life. Mitch thought, *I'm no murderer. But if I bug out it's not the same as killing her.* He was just shaping words in his skull; he knew there was no possibility of convincing himself of that.

Floyd said with quiet insinuation, "You're a gentleman, Mitch, and that's a tragic thing because nobody has much use for gentlemen any more. Nobody but Miss Conniston."

"So you'll just split and leave me holding the bag. Either I let Theodore kill her or I save her life so she can identify me to the cops. That's a sweet choice." He had been watching the girl; now he turned to face Floyd. "I've been in hock once. You're making a mistake if you think I'm willing to go back to it."

"What if I give you the plastic surgeon's name and address?"

"That'd make a difference," he conceded. "What is it?"

Floyd considered him. Finally he lifted his shoulders and let them drop. "No skin off my nose, I suppose. His name is von Roon. Gerhard von Roon. In a town called Caborca, in Sonora. Think you'll remember that?"

"I don't think I'll forget it. But how do I know you're telling the truth?"

Floyd smiled again. "You have my word. A figure of speech, of course—my word's worthless." His smile hardened suddenly like a scar. "Quit agonizing, my fine buffoon. You haven't got any choice at all—and you know it."

"You've thought of everything, haven't you?"

"Everything." Floyd walked past him, across the room to the girl; he stood above her, looking across her at Theodore, who stood against Billie Jean near the door. Floyd picked up the tape-recorder and said, "I'm going to make a phone call. It'll take me about an hour and I don't want anybody getting on anybody's nerves, Theodore."

"Why pick me out?"

"You know. Just remember I don't appreciate being displeased."

Georgie at the far end of the room said softly, "Floyd?"

"Later. When I get back." Floyd slung the recorder by its strap over his shoulder and went to the door. "Put the light out, Mitch."

Mitch extinguished the oil lamp. There was a faint rectangle of brief light as the door squeaked open and Floyd went out. Mitch lit the lamp again. He heard the crunch of Floyd's shoes, the slam of the car door in the barn across the street, the grind and catch of the engine. The car backed out and rolled away, not hurrying. Theodore blinked his good eye toward the door and settled down on his haunches like a Neanderthal in a cave and Mitch went over to Terry Conniston and said in a voice meant to carry no farther than her ears, "Look, I want to explain ——"

"Why?" she interrupted coldly. "I'm not interested."

"You're a cool one. When do you warm up?"

"When I see you fry." She hissed the words and turned her face away. He touched her arm; she was stiff in protest.

An earth-colored lizard skittered across the floor. Mitch got to his feet and moved a few yards away, bent down and pretended to busy himself sorting the canned food and drinks from the knapsacks. The girl's sulky silence ragged him; at least he wanted her gratitude.

Theodore and Billie Jean sat down together, talked in low tones. Theodore was looking at her abundant breasts, not smiling, talking earnestly. Billy Jean pouted with her heavy childish mouth, arguing with soft lips. She was an amazing creature: she lived for sensation, she exuded an unsubtle air of loosed amoral sexuality. When she caught Mitch watching her she lowered one shoulder to slip her dress-strap down and squeezed her right breast in her hand, aiming it at Mitch's face. "Right in your eye, Mitch." She laughed.

Mitch felt his face color. He looked away. In the food knapsack he found a batch of utensils wrapped in a plastic bag. He took out the kitchen knife and ran his thumb along its serrated blade. With a glance at Theodore he slipped the knife into his belt and went over to sit against the wall beside the sulky beautiful girl. She didn't look at him, even when he said lamely, "You see, Miss Conniston, our trouble is we can't relate to our environment." He tried to laugh.

CHAPTER **Seven**

Carl Oakley's bedroom was obliquely across the hall from Conniston's office. At nine thirty Oakley was walking toward the bedroom. It was early but the evening had been too strained; he had made his apologies and left the front room. Conniston walked with him as far as the office, saying he had paperwork to catch up on. Conniston stopped him outside the office door and said, "Can't stand that sonofabitch."

"Then throw him out," Oakley said, curt and irritable.

"No. Question is, how to get rid of him without Louise exploding. He's her guest, not mine."

"Why don't you explain it to her? Just tell her you can't stand him."

Conniston shook his big head. "Not that simple. She'd only throw tantrum, complain that I——"

In the office, the phone rang, cutting him off. Conniston cursed the interruption but strode into the office and picked up the phone from the desk and barked, "Yes?"

Oakley thought, *That's no way to answer a phone.* Conniston was surely crumbling. Morose, Oakley began to turn away; but he had a glimpse of Conniston, the big man's face changing and losing color, and he paused to look back. Conniston slumped against the desk, pressing the receiver against his ear. His eyes were round; his mouth was slack; his hand reached the desk and gripped its edge. Abruptly Conniston covered the mouthpiece with his hand and barked, "Extension. Quick!"

Oakley wheeled across the hall into his bedroom and picked up the extension phone.

Terry's voice came over the wire like a phonograph record being played on an old machine—distant and scratchy, without body.

"...got a gun. One of them wants to kill me so I won't be able to identify them. Please, Daddy."

There was silence for a stretching interval, although the connection hadn't been broken. Conniston's taut voice, startlingly loud, blasted Oakley's ear from the receiver: "Hello? Hello?"

The voice that came on the line was cool, without feeling— almost mechanical. "I played it over twice so you'd remember it, Mr. Conniston. You understand?"

"You fucking bastard," Conniston breathed. "What do you want?"

"Money, Mr. Conniston."

"Who are you?"

"I like to think of myself as a tax collector of sorts—separating money from people who've got too much of it, if you see what I——"

"Who are you?"

"Oh come on, Conniston, you don't really expect an answer to that, do you? Quit stalling for time—you can't trace this call anyway, take my word for it. Now I want half a million dollars in cash. Get it together tomorrow and wait for instructions and please don't insult me by trying to mark the money. No infrared inking, no consecutive numbers, no radioactive powder. I know all the tricks better than you do and I know how to test for them. Your daughter won't be turned loose until I'm satisfied the money's clean. Get it by tomorrow afternoon. Do I make myself understood?"

"Can't possibly get that much cash tomorrow. You're a fool."

"I think you can."

"Fifty thousand, maybe. Not more."

"Are you *really* willing to haggle over Terry's life? My, my. I want half a million dollars—and it's a seller's market."

"A drunk wants ten-year-old Scotch whiskey too but he'll

settle for forty-nine-cent wine if he has to."

Oakley, listening, couldn't believe his ears. Conniston must be mad. Pulsebeat drummed in Oakley's temples; he gripped the phone with aching knuckles.

The voice on the phone said mildly, "Your courage does you no justice, Mr. Conniston. It comes from ignorance. When you calm down you'll be forced to agree. The wages of sin are considerably above union scale, I'm afraid, and you'll just have to pay for my sins this time around. Now, if there are any——"

"Listen here," Conniston said, his voice braying loud.

"Let me finish."

"No. *You* let *me* finish. You harm a hair on her head and I'll spend last cent I own to see you killed. Clear?"

"Sure. Don't worry about it. She'll be fine—you just pony up on demand, all right?"

"You're asking too much. It's not possible."

"What you don't ask for you don't get. You'll make it possible, Mr. Conniston—I have every confidence in you."

"*Wait.* How do I know she's still alive? How do I know you didn't kill her after tape-recording?"

"I anticipated that, of course. Now, if there are any questions you'd like to ask her—questions to which only she could know the answers—give them to me and I'll relay them to her. We'll tape-record her answers and you'll hear the tapes when I get back to you with instructions for the ransom drop. Satisfactory?"

"Of course it's not satisfactory! I want——"

"Who cares what you want?" The voice was slow and as viscous as slow-rolling oil. "Quit sputtering and give me the questions."

"I'll find you. I'll have your guts for guitar strings."

"Sure, Mr. Conniston. I'm going to hang up now unless you want to give me the questions."

Conniston's voice dropped, beaten. "What she said to me when I built the swimming pool. And the nickname I always call her."

"Now you're using your head. Listen—no police, no FBI, nobody. I spot any snoopers sniffing around and you'll never see Terry again. Clear? Have the money with you, at home, tomorrow afternoon. You'll hear from me."

Click.

Oakley rang off and walked to the office like a somnambulist. Conniston still had the phone in his hand; he was reaching across the desk to switch off his tape-recorder, which he had installed six months ago to record all phone conversations automatically—part of his growing paranoid pattern.

Conniston said in a breaking voice, "Get Orozco."

Oakley took the receiver out of his hand and hung it up. "We'd better talk first."

"Get Orozco. Then we'll talk."

Oakley thought better of further argument; it would do no harm to call Orozco. He dialed the area code and number, not needing to look it up; a woman answered on the fourth ring.

"Maria? Carl Oakley. *Es necesario que yo hable con Diego, pronto por favor.*"

"*Seguro que sí—momento.*" She was laughing at his ungrammatical Spanish. He could hear an infant yowling in the background.

Waiting, he gave Conniston his covert scrutiny. The big man was kneading his knuckles; his eyes flashed and darted like fireworks.

"Hello, Carl. *Com' está?*"

"Diego, can you get down here right now? Earle Conniston's ranch."

"Right-now-tonight?"

"Yes. Hire a plane."

"I guess. I was planning a good night's sleep but I suppose it's urgent?"

"As urgent as it can get."

"Okay. You'll get a hell of a bill from me."

"Just get yourself an airplane. We'll expect you in a couple hours—I'll have somebody set out landing lights on the field."

"All righty. See you."

Oakley broke the connection and dialed 423 on the intercom circuit. When the bunkhouse answered he gave instructions to have the landing field lighted and to meet Orozco with a jeep. Then he hung up and turned a reluctant face to Conniston.

Conniston's eyes looked like two holes burned in cloth.

"Suppose they're watching the ranch. They'll see the plane—maybe think it's the FBI."

"Want me to call him back and cancel?"

"No. To hell with it. I need a drink." Conniston bolted out of the office, voice trailing back: "Stay by the phone."

Left alone, Oakley felt chilled. He chewed a cigar to shreds, enraged beyond reason by his feeling of helplessness. The hot fury sawed through him until his jaw muscles stood out like cables and he wanted to plunge his fist through the desk, the wall, anything in reach.

Conniston returned with two tall glasses full of whiskey and ice. He handed one over and Oakley accepted it without remark. Conniston was chewing up an ice cube the way a dog would grind up a bone—with loud cracking noises. Oakley watched him with dulled curiosity: Conniston went deliberately around the desk to his chair, sat, planted both elbows on the desk, steepled his fingers and squinted—the picture of rational calm. Somehow in the short moments to the bar and back he had got a grip on himself. He looked as he used to look when faced with a business decision: thoughtful, weighing the issues, not ready to jump to conclusions, not prepared to be easily swayed.

The essential coldness which Conniston's behavior revealed was more frightening to Oakley than panic. Conniston said slowly, "Think they've got a hammerlock on me. Fucking terrorists think they can do it. Well, they can't."

"The hell they can't. They have."

"No. I'm not as soft as they think. Don't count on me throwing my hand in."

"What are you talking about?"

"Think they can wipe their feet on me," Conniston muttered.

Oakley's face changed. "I wouldn't worry about that right now. We've got other things to think about. I'll have to call Farmers and Merchants in the morning, think of some reasonable explanation for wanting that much untraceable cash—and just hope they've got that much on hand."

"You'd pay the bastards then?"

"For God's sake what option have you got? Of course we'll

pay. Anything—anything beyond reason, of course. There's no choice at all."

"Wrong," Conniston said. His head did not move; only his eyes shifted toward Oakley. "What if we refuse?"

Oakley stared at him. "You can't mean that."

"Maybe. Let's think it out."

"There'd be hell to pay."

"Then we'll pay it."

"No. It's Terry who'd have to pay."

"You understand things too quickly, Carl. Just stop and think. What if we refused to pay?"

"How can you even ask that?"

"To find out what the answer is. Well?"

"What do *you* think would happen? For God's sake, it's as plain as the nose on your face!"

"Saying they'd kill her?"

"Of course they would!"

Conniston shook his head. His pouched eyes were fiery. "Not unless they planned to kill her anyway. Follow me?"

"No. I don't. What you're saying has got a smell of sickness to it."

"What I'm saying," Conniston answered evenly, "either they're killers or they're not. If they're killers, they'll kill her whether we pay or not—she's seen their faces. If they're not killers, whole thing's a bluff."

"Certainly—but how could you possibly take that chance?"

"You don't get this yet, do you? Our whole objective is to save Terry, right? Not to do what *they* want just because they ask. Now, question: given choice between no money but freedom, and big money but inevitable capture, what will *they* do? Look —spell it out. They call tomorrow. I give them choice, starting with premise that I'm a man of limitless wealth. My offer: they turn Terry loose, she returns here unharmed, and we'll forget whole thing. The only other choice I offer—since I refuse to pay ransom—is for them to kill her and make run for it. But if they choose that course they recognize I'll spend every last cent of my vast fortune to see them dead—tracked down no matter how many dollars and years it takes, found, captured, and put to death by most painful slow method imaginable. Given those alternatives, and no others, which would you choose?"

Oakley stared with awed disbelief. "You'd actually take that risk with Terry's life at stake?"

He saw color rise in Conniston's cheeks. "You just don't get it, do you? Carl, God damn it, *that* risk is far less than the risk we face—the risk she faces—if we do it their way! Can't you understand that? Because there is no way to guarantee they'll keep word after we pay ransom. No way to assure Terry's safety whether or not we pay. Risk is same either way—therefore why pay? Much better to scare shit out of them. Fear can always be used against terrorists. Nothing else will work. Jesus, man, can't you see? I don't give *that* for the money. I want Terry's life—and I believe this is wisest course. When you face two risks you choose the less dangerous one. That's all I'm saying."

"You can't actually believe what you're saying."

"I have to."

"What kind of maniac are you?"

"You can't shout me down, Carl. Don't try. If I can't make you see that——"

"You can't. Stop it. You act as if you're dealing with an opposition team of corporate businessmen who can be reasoned with. You heard that voice on the phone. These people are of another species. There's no reasoning with psychopaths. That voice belonged to a man who's lacked from birth the ability to distinguish right from wrong. We're dealing with a monster who's indifferent to fear just as he's indifferent to cruelty."

"Possibly. But if you read that much into his voice, and read it right, then he plans to kill her anyway. Paying ransom won't stop him."

Abrupt and distressed, Oakley threw back his head to swallow a mouthful of whiskey. Ice cubes in the glass shot forward and whacked his upper lip. He said desperately, "All right, suppose you do this and they call your bluff. Suppose you spend every cent you've got to track them down and see them killed. When you do, Carl—when you do, what then?"

"That is not my intent."

"Who cares what you intended? Who's going to care what your real motives were? Earle, you're judged by the consequences of your acts, not by your intent. If you go through with this——"

"Yes?"

"You'll have to defend it for a hell of a long time," Oakley finished weakly. "Or try to."

"Only thing that matters now is Terry. I couldn't care less about future accusations and justifications." Conniston showed his contempt. "I'm not concerned with being judged. Concerned with my daughter's life." The clipped words bounced harshly around the room. His glass stood sweating on the desk; he reached for it and drank, his eyes dismal; his mask of authority had sagged but in its place was stubborn resolve—the big jaw had crept forward belligerently, the hand on the desk was curled into a fist.

Oakley said bitterly, "At least talk it over with Louise before you decide to do it."

"Why? So she can take your side and try talk me out of it?"

"You assume she won't agree with you?"

"Of course."

"Why?"

"Automatic reaction. Sentimentality. Tradition—kidnap, pay ransom, last-reel magic rescue. She knows *The Desperate Hours* by heart but not much about reality."

"Reality," Oakley breathed, "is a psychopath out there somewhere with a gun pointed at Terry's head. You anticipate Louise will disagree with you—doesn't it occur to you that anybody at all would reject this mad scheme of yours, with good reason? How many people do you think you could find who——"

"God damn it," Conniston cut him off, "I'm not conducting popular-opinion poll!"

"Will you at least talk to Louise? You owe it to her to tell her what's happened, at the very least."

"She's not Terry's mother."

"She's your wife."

Conniston pushed his chair back. All his resistance seemed to have been channeled in one direction; he didn't argue this secondary point. "All right—I suppose." He got up and came around the desk. "Come with me. Want you with me when I break it to her."

"You think that's wise?"

Conniston gave him a strange look. "There was a time," he murmured, "when I thought I knew what wisdom was. Come on." He swung the door open and waited for Oakley.

Oakley's legs were not working well. They tramped to the front room but it was empty; one light burned in a lonely corner. "Gone to bed," Conniston judged, and heaved himself around. With sudden alarm Oakley hurried after him.

To Oakley's dismay Conniston didn't knock when he reached his wife's bedroom; he palmed the knob and pushed the door open without hesitation. Oakley wheeled inside in his wake, bitterly certain of what they would find.

Faint light splashed past them into the room from the open doorway and revealed the two figures naked on the bed. Louise's head was lifted, rigid with alarm; her tawny hair glistened faintly. The room smelled of cold cream and shampoo. Oakley was strangely, oppressively aware of the odor; as he was of the frozen tableau on the bed before Frankie Adams rolled over, his feral face turning vividly scarlet. Adams said with absurd aplomb, "Jesus Christ—look who's here. Listen, Earle, don't get sore—even the government frowns on monopoly, hey?" He uttered a hysterical shriek of laughter that beat strident echoes around the room. Louise's lips upturned in a cowardly apologetic half-smile; then, when Conniston moved, her face went flat and lifeless with horror.

Oakley reached out to stop Conniston but he was not fast enough. Conniston leaped for the bed with an inarticulate roar, batted Louise aside and snapped both hands around Adams' chicken-thin throat. Oakley rammed forward and tried to grab him but the two men rolled off the far side of the bed, locked together; Oakley tripped on bedclothes tangled in discard on the floor and fell across Louise, hearing her brief whimpering grunts of panic. Thunder roared in Oakley's ears. He kicked his feet free of the entangling sheets and hurled himself off the bed in a violent somersault, striking the wall with one shoe, coming down on one knee and both hands. He reached for a thrashing ankle—Adams'—but the foot whipped around against his wrist, stunning him up to the shoulder. Someone was crying out. He threw himself forward but a hard thing whipped out of the darkness—elbow or knee—bash against his temple.

His head rocked back; he fell over on his side, half under the bed. Numbed and throbbing, he reached sluggishly, squirming out from under, rolling his head to seek the others. He rolled over on his back and then he saw them above him, outlined against the open door.

They had got their feet under them somehow: Adam's thin naked arms whipped up and broke Conniston's hold on his throat; Conniston bawled a shrieking cry and swung an open-handed blow that sounded like the flat of a cleaver striking a side of beef.

It knocked Adams off the wall. Startlingly resilient, the comedian bounced acrobatically and drop-kicked the big man, both bare feet into Conniston's belly. Conniston pitched back, lost his balance, toppled back toward the brass bedposts at the foot of the bed. The back of his head struck the brass globe with a dull, sickening sound. Bones jerking, he flopped down and slid to the floor.

Oakley got his legs under him. His knees trembled when he rushed past the foot of the bed and pinned Adams against the wall with a stiff arm. "All right," he panted. "Stop it!"

Louise lay on her elbows, looking down over the foot of the bed. She made retching sounds in her throat. Adams said with stifled alarm, "Okay, okay, get off me."

Conniston was crumpled, not moving. Oakley turned the comedian loose and dropped to the floor beside Conniston. He slipped a hand under Conniston's head to support it—felt a wet pulpy cavity, removed his hand to see a dark smear across it. Swallowing spasmically he reached for Conniston's wrist. The pulse stopped beating under his hand.

Adams' voice reached him dimly through the thudding in his ears: "Call the doctor. *Quick!*"

"No," Oakley heard himself say. "Don't call anybody." Later he would remember that and ask himself why he had said it.

He dragged himself to his feet. Adams whispered, "Dead?" And when no one answered him, he said, "Sweet, sweet Jesus."

In that moment Oakley glanced suddenly at Louise and caught on her features in that unguarded instant a look of savage joyful satisfaction. It was gone so swiftly he might have imagined it.

"He's dead." He pronounced the fact with harsh clarity. "He's dead."

CHAPTER **Eight**

Oakley sat in Conniston's huge office chair, rocking, withdrawn deep in himself, watching the others' faces change as they listened to the playback of the tape-recorded phone call from the kidnaper. He saw the different grip fear took on each of their faces: Louise—placid, wooden, blindly stunned, staring sightless at the slow-spinning tape reels; Frankie Adams—tremble-lipped, white, ghastly, eyes brimming with despair, ready to burst into tears; Diego Orozco—big-rumped and tub-bellied, sitting on a straight chair with both hands on his knees, staring at the floor with intense concentration.

The muscles of Oakley's arms and back still throbbed from the limp deadweight of Earle Conniston's corpse: he had carried it, undressed and wrapped in a tarp, to the deep-freeze, with great care—*Odd how gently we treat people after they're dead.* He felt slightly anesthetized, as if the tactile nerve-endings of his extremities had lost their sensitivity: dreamlike. Yet his mind worked with heightened clarity, as it sometimes did when he was overtired; often inspirations had struck him late at night on the point of falling asleep—this hour was like that, his mind racing, uninhibited by ordinary daytime commonplaces, running fast and smooth like an engine disengaged from its load.

He let the tape play through to its finish. There followed Diego Orozco's short grunt. No one else spoke until Oakley stirred and heard his own voice issue from his chest with cool precision: "That's why we can't let it be known outside this room that Earle's dead. If the kidnaper finds out I wouldn't give two cents for Terry's chances. Diego?"

"Sure. You're dead right."

Cataleptic immobility was Louise Conniston's only response. She wore a nylon negligee, carelessly fastened; it clung electrically to her thrusting breasts. Her hair was in disarray, her face chalky. For the first time in Oakley's memory she was indifferent to her appearance. Sensitive to the others' eyes on her, she turned in her chair with a lurch, almost upsetting herself. Her face moved back and forth like some sort of wind-up toy—mechanically. It took Oakley a minute to realize she was shaking her head, rhythmically denying to herself that any of this had happened, that it could have happened. Oakley said in a harsh, cross voice intended to break past the barrier of her shock, "Quit rending your garments. Snap out of it."

Her face filled with venom. "Shut up."

"I need to have you lucid. You've got to pay attention."

"You need," she muttered with icy scorn.

Frankie Adams stood up like an old man and pulled tight the cloth belt of his dressing gown. "A drink would help."

"All right," Oakley said. "But nurse it."

Louise said, *"Can't you shut up?"*

"Don't shout," Oakley said. "I'm not deaf." His words had a dry rustle. Orozco went to Louise and picked up her hand and began to rub it and pat it between his big brown hams. Louise neither responded nor withdrew. Oakley left his chair and went out of the room with Frankie Adams, taking him down the hall to the dining room and standing in the doorway to watch Adams pour a shaky drink at the side bar. Adams said, "Want one?"

"No." He wanted a clear head.

Adams said, "Waiter, there's a fly in my soup," and sat down on a dining chair as though genuflecting. He looked up at Oakley and added morosely, "Check, please." His grin was a spasm of clenched teeth and drawn lips. Unable to hold Oakley's glance he shifted his eyes away and demolished half his drink. Oakley tipped his shoulder against the doorjamb and folded his arms, his eyes half-shuttered.

There was a stretching interval of silence during which Oakley's motionless scrutiny got on Adams' nerves as it was intended to do; Adams squirmed and said, "Look, God knows I didn't mean any of this to happen. How was I to know he'd come busting in on us? She said he hadn't been inside her bedroom in three months."

"You drop-kicked him like a pro. Where'd you learn that?"

"When you're a runt like me growing up on the Lower East Side you learn how to fight. Besides, I started out in a boardwalk carnival. Acrobatics."

"I thought as much."

"What's that supposed to mean?"

"I'm a lawyer. A little rusty on criminal code, maybe, but I seem to recall the special skills of certain athletes can be considered deadly weapons, legally. A prizefighter's fists, for example."

"You're saying——"

"I'm only speculating."

"You're trying to scare the shit out of me—and you're succeeding. Why?"

Oakley shook his head; he was still thinking. Adams broke into his thoughts: "You brought that fat greaser into this. Why?"

"Earle wanted him in."

"To handle the kidnaping?"

"Yes."

"How much you tell him about—about the way Earle Conniston died?"

"Enough."

"Who guarantees he won't blow the whistle?"

"Diego works for me. If anybody blows any whistles I'll be the one."

Adams flushed, poured a second drink, and said without the belligerent conviction the question required, "Since when did you get elected to give the orders here?"

"Do you want me to pick up the phone and tell the cops who killed Earle?"

Adams held his tongue. But Oakley pressed it: Adams had to be convinced. "What do you want to do, Frankie? Call in the police, tell them Earle caught his wife with her head on the wrong pillow and you killed him to keep the truth from getting out? Killed him with what might just be described by a sharp prosecutor as a deadly weapon—an acrobat's feet?"

"It wasn't like that! You know it wasn't like that!"

"Maybe. But if Louise and I get behind that version and stick to it, they'll put you away."

"Nuts. The sonofabitch came at me like a maniac. It was self-defense—an accident. It's your word against mine."

"Let's say it's the word of a bankrupt third-rate nightclub comic with a shady background against the word of a respected member of the bar and a multimillionaire widow. Whose story would you believe if you were on the jury?"

"Bastard," Adams hissed without strength. "You want a fall guy and I'm it, hey? Let's hear it for Frankie Adams, lez an gennulmen, Frankie Adams the ten-carat loser. Jesus H. Christ."

"It doesn't have to be that way."

"You've got it all set up. Go ahead and pull the rope."

"No. There's another way to play it. Unless you *want* to drag a scandalous mess through the courts and the newspapers and end up with your head in a sack."

"What are you, kidding?"

"Which way do you want it?"

"What choice have I got?"

"Suppose you and I and Louise were sitting in the front room playing cards when we heard a thud from the back of the house. Suppose we went back to investigate and found Earle had tripped over the rug and fallen and hit the back of his head on the bedpost. Suppose we tell that story and I have a doctor sign the death certificate accidental death."

Adams sat slack-jawed, watching him warily. "Where you figure to find a doctor to sign something like that?"

"Big money can buy a few harmless lies—and a lot of silence. How about it, Frankie?"

Adams tucked his chin in toward his shoulder like a shy schoolboy trying to remember the answer to a teacher's question. "What do I have to do?"

"I'll let you know. In the meantime you don't say a word to

anyone about anything unless you clear it with me first. Fair enough?"

"Listen, the first time I got jumped by three big kids in the playground I learned not to fight a squeeze. Don't worry about me."

"I won't," Oakley said, and gave him a synthetic smile utterly devoid of trust.

He shepherded Adams back to the office. Louise looked better; there was color in her face and when he crossed the room her eyes followed his movements alertly. Her hands gripped the arms of her chair tightly.

Oakley settled into Earle's chair and veiled his eyes and spoke in a soft voice which eased up against the cork-lined walls and was immediately absorbed:

"We've all heard the tape. I've told you what Earle wanted to do. I think he was dead wrong but we'll see. Diego, what about the tape?"

"I just played it back again. I think the sonabitch meant business. You asking my advice? Usually, a snatch caper like this, you get the cops and the FBI and they tell you to follow instructions and pay the ransom. Rule of thumb is you got a better chance to get the victim back alive if you pay the ransom and don' rock the boat."

"Rock the boat," Adams mumbled, incredulous. "Christ, the boat's already sunk."

Oakley ignored him; he said to Orozco, "I get a feeling your next word will be 'But.'"

"Yeah. She said one of them wants to kill her so she won't be able to identify them. Does that mean she's seen all their faces? Or have they got her blindfolded but one of them wants insurance anyway? She knows their voices."

Louise said, "What difference does that make?"

"Could make a lot, lady. If they keep her blindfolded and she don't see their faces, maybe they really expect to let loose of her after it's over. But if they never even bothered to blindfold her it's a whole different enchilada."

Oakley shook his head. "We'll probably have to make our

decision without the answer to that question. What about trying to trace the phone calls?"

Orozco's fleshy dark cheeks sagged. "Maybe—maybe. First thing in the morning I'll get a tap on the line. These new computer exchanges, sometimes you can get a real fast trace on a call if you're ready for it. I can get a crew of operatives stand ready to move on signal. Beyond that I just don' know. You people got to make your own decision about the ransom. I only say this—was it my daughter I wouldn't take the chance Conniston was going to take. I'd play it by the book whether you bring in cops or not. They'd tell you to play it by the book, believe me."

"You mean pay the ransom?" Louise asked.

"Yeah. I mean pay the ransom."

Frankie Adams said, "Isn't there any other way we could start trying to get a line on them?"

Orozco made a face. "Few honnerd thousand people in this half of Arizona. Where you going to start? That guy on the phone sounded too smart to give away any clues we could use. We got nothing to go on."

Louise sat up straight. "All of you are forgetting one little thing."

The determined quiet of her tone drew Oakley's full attention. Louise looked from face to face; finally she said, "None of you is in any position to decide what's to be done with Earle's money. That money belongs to Terry and me. We're his heirs."

Oakley closed his eyes down to slits. "You're saying you don't want to pay the ransom?"

"I'm saying I think maybe Earle was right. Maybe we'll stand a better chance by not paying—by frightening them instead."

"In other words," Oakley murmured, "Terry's not worth half a million dollars to you."

"You make me sound cold-blooded. You know I don't mean that. The chances are if we pay the ransom we lose both Terry and the money. What's the good of that?"

Oakley bounced to his feet; the backs of his knees knocked the big swivel-chair back against the wall. "Don't even think about it, Louise."

"Are you threatening me?" she demanded.

"If you like. I'll remind you a criminal forfeits any right to the proceeds of his crime. If you're found guilty of being accessory to your husband's murder you won't inherit a dime—regardless of whether Terry's alive or dead."

Her eyes popped at him. "Convicted of——? You can't be serious!"

"Think about it. An able prosecutor smooth-talking a jury. The young wife of the old millionaire, the wife's boy friend—both conspiring to murder the old man and live happily ever after on his millions. Strike a chord?"

"It was nothing of the kind." Her face turned crimson; she looked down at her hands. "What you must think of me."

Oakley said, "Don't misunderstand. What I'm saying is that if the circumstances of Earle's death ever become public knowledge the newspapers will wallow in it and the classic explanation I've just suggested is the first thing they'll assume. You'll be dragged through slime—it's the kind of case that'll be tried and judged by the press long before it ever gets near a courtroom. Is that what you want? Or would you rather none of it ever got into print? Would you rather be grilled mercilessly by a prosecuting attorney hell-bent on making a big reputation at your expense or get scot-free after a few perfunctory routine questions by a bored county official? Would you rather have Earle's death dragged through the front pages as murder or manslaughter, or have it appear quietly in a black box on the obituary page as an accidental death? Yes, damn it, I *am* threatening you."

She studied his face; she glanced at Adams and at Orozco; she said tentatively, "The penalty for blackmail is damned severe, Carl."

"Ten to twenty years," Frankie Adams said dryly. "Felony."

Oakley shook his head. "Am I trying to extort a penny from you? Come off it. I'm trying to get Terry back and I believe the only way to do it is to pay the ransom. I'm using the only weapon I've got."

Louise sank back in her chair. "I suppose I've got no choice."

"Then you agree to meet the kidnapers' demands?"

"If you think it's best." She had given up.

Orozco's voice rolled between them abruptly: "This here weapon of yours looks to me like the kind of stick you use to beat dead horses with, Carl. Maybe this all hit you too fast to think it out, but how do you figure to raise the ransom money with Conniston dead? And who's going to make contact with the kidnaper when he calls back and wants to talk to Conniston? He ain't likely willing to talk to anybody else."

"He won't have to," Oakley said.

Louise, full of acid, snapped, "I suppose you're going to reincarnate him?"

"In a way. In the morning Earle Conniston's going to call the president of Farmers and Merchants and arrange to have the cash ready for me to pick it up. In the afternoon when the kidnaper calls back Earle Conniston's going to answer the phone."

Looking past her astonished disbelieving face, he saw slow comprehension spread across Frankie Adams' narrow features. Oakley said relentlessly, "I've heard you do Conniston's voice. Nobody will know the difference, especially over a telephone. You're going to be Earle Conniston."

Adams shot bolt upright in his chair, ready to rise—but Oakley's eyes jammed him back down in his seat.

"You've got to be out of your gourd," Adams said.

"You can do it."

"Count me out. Nuts."

Oakley just looked at him patiently until Adams began to squirm, remembering the earlier conversation; Adams seemed to grow smaller and heavier in the chair. "Look, I'll try it if I have to but I'm in no shape to do a convincing act. Besides, there's too many holes in it—it's no good. We can't keep Conniston alive forever, can we? What happens when they find out we concealed his death?"

"I'll take care of that. Nobody's going to find out."

"Maybe so. Maybe so. But Christ, I can't even remember what he sounded like."

"I'm sure Mrs. Conniston's willing to coach you." He ignored Louise's sarcastic glance; he added, "If it matters you'll be paid for the performance."

"A bribe, you mean."

"Enough to keep body and soul apart," Oakley agreed with a thin smile. "Maybe it'll encourage you to work on it. I want you to practice voice and delivery until you've got it letter-perfect."

"Easy for you to say—but what the hell, when I got here I was just about ready to go out on the street with a tin cup, that's no secret. How much I get paid?"

"I won't haggle. Say ten thousand."

Louise said, "Whose money are you slinging around like that?"

He didn't answer her. Adams said, "Only one thing. I wish I could be sure I can trust you."

"None of us can afford *not* to trust each other," Oakley replied. "And don't forget Terry. She's got to trust us too."

After a while Adams said abstractedly, "He talked like an obstacle race. Didn't he? Left out articles and subjects of sentences. Voice a little like Gregory Peck, deep in the diaphragm. Christ, I guess I'll have a hack at it."

When the sun burst through the window Adams was practicing Conniston's voice, listening to Oakley's remarks: how to talk to the banker, the name of the banker's wife about whom Conniston always asked, the ostensible reason for raising so much unmarked cash—a big under-the-table payment to secure the cooperation of key stockholders in a corporate takeover. Oakley took him over it a dozen times; when he left Adams with Louise and Orozco he had a taut feeling of expectant confidence. He went back to the bedroom to shower and shave and change into fresh clothes. When he checked his watch it was shortly after eight—ten o'clock New York time. He called a stockbroker in Phoenix and kept his voice low: "How many shares of Conniston stock do I hold? How many shares outstanding? . . . All right. Sell two hundred thousand shares short for me. . . . Never mind that. Do it through dummies—scatter it so it won't look like a power play. I'm not trying to manipulate it but I expect it to go down a few points and I want to make a few bucks, that's all. Breathe one word to anybody and I'll make it hurt, Fred."

Afterward he immediately called another broker in Los Angeles and repeated the substance of the conversation; he repeated the short-sell order with half a dozen brokers across the country before he rang off and turned toward the front of the house, walking briskly on crepe-soled shoes, and saw Orozco looming darkly in the corridor. The fat man, vigilant and silent, held his troubled glance until Oakley felt uncomfortable enough to look away. When he came up, Orozco said mildly, "I went to call my boys to get working on the wiretap call-trace but you were on the line." There was no hint of guile on Orozco's dark bland cheeks. But Oakley knew he had heard the whole thing.

"Just keep it to yourself, Diego. It'll be worth your while."

"I'm sure it will," Orozco murmured, and turned heavily back into the office. Oakley had to steel himself against the sound coming out of the office—Earle Conniston's voice.

CHAPTER **Nine**

Terry Conniston sat like a taut-wound watch spring in the shade of the sagging porch overhang. Near the perilous breaking-edge, she felt as if at any moment she might start screaming and not be able to stop; and so she kept herself rigidly under control, all her movements slow and cautious, all her decisions ponderous. Her slender fingers clenched and opened at regular intervals; she watched a domed anthill which squatted naked like a cancerous boil on the face of the ground below the porch. The brutal little monsters had denuded the surrounding earth of everything but rocks and sand.

Overhead little gray birds flitted soundlessly from rooftop to rooftop and the indifferent sun burned down like brass; the desert heat was thick and close. The young sandy-haired one called Mitch sat against the wall at the far corner of the porch, making a point of not watching her. His face was not cruel like the others'; he seemed willing to respect her desire to be left alone. At first she had been surprised by the casual way they had of keeping desultory watch on her but not confining her at all. Only gradually had it dawned on her that since she didn't have keys to either car her only means of escape would be afoot across the desert, and they would be able to see her on the flats anywhere within a mile of the ghost town. It was a far more effective prison than bars.

About noon by the sun, with a look compounded of the irascible and the hangdog, Mitch uncoiled his length and went inside, leaving her alone. She didn't stir. In a little while he returned with an army-style mess kit of cold food out of cans, handed it to her without a word and went back to his post.

Floyd, the dark evil one, came out and stood on the porch and stretched like a cat. When he glanced at her she felt mesmerized by his cold eyes. Floyd had a driving, brutal, elemental thrust of granite personality. His magnetism, in spite of it, was uncanny—repellent and fascinating at once: the charismatic impact of raw unshielded masculinity, erotic and frightening.

The pulse throbbed at Terry's throat. She addressed herself to her meal, keenly aware that Floyd was watching her with cynical vicious amusement.

The girl, Billie Jean, appeared behind Floyd, filling the caved-in doorway with her body, all meaty thighs and bovine lactic breasts which bobbed and surged with her movements. She studied Floyd's back for a while before she stepped out and passed Floyd with a slow flirt of the shoulder, grinning. Floyd casually reached out and rubbed her breast. "You're a fire hazard, Billie Jean." It made her laugh.

"How about a jab in the fun hole, Floyd?"

"Later—later."

Disappointed, Billie Jean moved away, dropping off the porch into the sunshine and wandering aimlessly up the street. Floyd said, "Stay close."

"I ain't going nowhere," she said petulantly.

"If you hear an airplane or a car duck inside a building and stay out of sight."

"I know," she pouted, and ambled away.

Floyd turned toward Mitch and spoke as if Terry weren't there: "I'm going to make a phone call, arrange for the drop. Keep things under control."

"What if I can't?"

"That's up to you," Floyd said. "If you fall you break, Mitch. Law of gravity." His unrevealing eyes touched Terry briefly; his mouth smiled frighteningly and then, according to his bewildering intricacy of thought, it was time to go: he jumped catlike from the porch and trotted across the street into the barn.

Shortly he came out, driving the dusty Oldsmobile, and put it into the central powder of the street, rumbling away.

In the stretching quiet that followed, an overwhelming anxiety slowly poisoned what was left of Terry's willed patience. Unable to remain still any longer she got up. Her knees felt weak. She stepped hesitantly toward the edge of the porch, waiting to see how Mitch would respond. He didn't get up; only his head turned to indicate his interest in her movements. She stepped down into the sunshine and walked very slowly along the street.

She had gone twenty or thirty paces when Mitch caught up with her. He didn't touch her; he fell into step beside her and said, "I hope you don't mind if I walk along with you."

A sharp report rose to her lips but died stillborn. When she looked at him, his eyes were kind. She thought, *I need any friends I can get.* Yet in the back of her mind she couldn't help thinking of stories she had heard about policemen and confidence men and spies—evil men working in teams, one partner softening you up with friendliness while the other stood ready to pounce. She couldn't see what they stood to gain by that kind of tactic in her case but just the same she couldn't begin to trust Mitch. He was, after all, one of them.

She searched his face with an odd intensity. "You hate him, don't you?"

"He makes it easy." Neither of them mentioned Floyd's name; it wasn't necessary. Mitch said, "For seven cents he'd hang his own mother on a meathook."

"Then why are you here?"

"To keep you alive." He laughed dispiritedly. "This wasn't my idea, this kidnaping thing. I want you to know that. I tried to stop them from doing it. Well, maybe I didn't try all that hard, but I didn't want them to. I wanted to get away. I didn't want anything to do with it."

The words tumbled out of him. She said afterward, "I'd like to believe you but you're here. You haven't run away. Nothing's stopping *you.*"

"You are," he said. "If I bug out who's left to keep Theodore away from you?"

She held herself rigidly aloof from him. "You don't know how much I want to believe you. But——"

She didn't finish it, and Mitch said dryly, "Yeah." They went on, twenty yards in silence. "Well," Mitch said awkwardly, and trailed off again. Then suddenly he stopped and frowned at her. "You worry me. You're not behaving according to Freud."

"Having hysterics, you mean? I'm on the verge of it, believe me." She stepped closer to him and glanced back toward the mercantile. No one was in sight. "He terrifies me, honest to God. The weight of his eyes can buckle you—that horrible cold look of his. Is there *anything* we can do?"

"It's hard to talk to Floyd. He listens to his own little voices —the line's always busy."

"He's filth," she said furiously. When she tilted her face down her hair swung out languorously; she brushed it back and laughed dispiritedly. "I'm putting myself on, aren't I? Clutching at straws."

"What straws?"

"Hoping for a minute that you were on my side."

"I am," he said. "But I don't know what to do about it."

"We could run for it. Both of us—right now."

"Fat chance." He was looking back the way they had come. When she followed the direction of his glance she saw the two men standing on the porch—Georgie in his candy-striped shirt; Theodore, tugging at a thick black hair in his nostril. They were watching with fully focused attention. Mitch said, "We'd better get back before Theodore decides to start something. Like find out how much of a beating I can take."

"Would he?"

"Sure."

"Why?"

"Who knows. He gets uptight easy. Sometimes he doesn't remember things from one hour to the next but when it comes to grudges and sex he's got a one-track mind like an elephant. Only he doesn't think with it. He thinks with his fists."

"Has he got a grudge against you?"

"More than one. For one thing he thinks he'd like to—well, wrestle you a little, you know?"

Rape me is what you mean. She folded her arms and hugged herself, flashing a quick furtive scrutiny at Theodore on the porch, trying to catch some hint of expression on his asymmetrical crippled face.

Mitch was still talking:

"He could use a few inhibitions. I don't think he's got any at all. The only thing that's slowing him down is I've got this crummy kitchen knife in my belt and he's not too sure how good I am with it. He knows he can take me regardless but he doesn't want to get carved up in the process."

"How good are you with it?"

"Probably lousy. The only thing I've ever used a knife for was peeling potatoes. Fortunately he doesn't know that. But he keeps gnashing his teeth and sooner or later he'll boil over and try something. He hates everybody—it's only a matter of degree, it doesn't take much—if your face isn't all mangled and scarred up like his that's enough to make him hate you, by itself."

Terry shuddered involuntarily. They were walking very slowly back toward the store. On the porch Georgie Rymer said something to Theodore and turned back inside with a quick over-the-shoulder look, like the hasty bright-eyed glance of a heister peddling hot wristwatches near a traffic cop. Theodore watched him disappear, then pulled his head around toward Mitch and Terry. He had large greasy pores on his nose. His one good eye was bold and fierce. She glanced at Mitch and saw sweat burst out in beads on his upper lip.

When they reached the porch Mitch took the initiative, throwing Theodore off balance: "You let him go inside by himself—he's probably rooting around trying to find the dope where Floyd hid it. You know Floyd told you not to let him alone in there."

Taken aback, Theodore canceled whatever it was he had intended to say. He rolled his tongue around his misshapen lips; she saw spittle run from his mouth. He said, "Shit," and wheeled inside, ducking to clear the fallen beam.

Mitch's face hardened, bleak and guarded. He made a half-hearted signal with his head; Terry obeyed, returning to her place at the corner of the porch and sitting down. Georgie came out with Theodore right behind him; Theodore said crossly, "He wasn't noplace near it."

Georgie had a cunning look on his face; he turned an innocent glance on Mitch but his eyes were at odds with his lips. The three men stood in an awkward triangle for an intolerable length of time before Georgie stirred nervously and said, "I got to"—and glanced at her with a tentative smile—"relieve myself?"

Theodore's eye rolled toward Terry. She tried to ignore him. He said to Mitch, "Okay. You better go with him."

Theodore fixed her with what passed for a smile. She held her breath until Mitch said, "I guess not," and slowly went past Theodore to the inside of the porch, where he put his shoulder blades against the wall and hooked both thumbs in his pockets. "You go with him if you think he can't do it for himself."

"It ain't that," Theodore said. "He needs watching."

"What for?"

"He just does."

"Then watch him yourself."

Georgie said waspishly, "I don't need no nursemaid," and walked off the porch. He hurried up the street toward a half-crumpled shack. Theodore made as if to follow him, but changed his mind. He circled toward Mitch—and stopped, frowning, as if he had forgotten what he was going to say. He shook his head in exasperation. Looking past Mitch he spotted Billie Jean up the street, making circles in the dust with the toe of her shoe, and abruptly Theodore swung that way, saying out of the side of his mouth, "Both of you stay put."

Terry let her breath out. When Mitch came over to her and sat down she had to fight down the impulse to burst out wailing. She drew her knees up and rested her chin on her knuckles and heard Mitch say as if he were a long distance away, "Ever have the feeling the world was falling down around your ankles?"

"That's not funny," she muttered.

"Sorry."

"I just can't stand it, sitting here—waiting. Not doing anything."

"I know."

"My car's right there in the barn. Couldn't we at least try——"

"Floyd has the keys in his pocket."

"Well, they hot-wire them or something, don't they? When they steal cars?"

"I wouldn't know how. Maybe if I had a couple hours I could figure it out if I didn't electrocute myself trying. But we couldn't walk from here to the barn without getting Theodore all over us."

"You're not a hell of a great big lot of help, you know that?" Her eyes filled and she blinked furiously.

"Look, I'm just as scared as you are. What do you want?" He gave her an angry look. "Damn it, cut that out. I don't know what to do when girls cry."

"I'm not crying."

"Oh. I suppose it's hay fever."

"Suppose what you like," she snapped. She sniffed and rubbed her eyes. "Oh, hell," she bawled softly. "Oh, hell and damn and shit. I don't want to be killed, Mitch. I want to *live.* Jesus, I want to get married and have kids and live in some little town someplace with a husband who comes home every night at five thirty and mows the lawn on weekends and every once in a while tells me how beautiful and cuddly I am."

She blew her nose. Mitch said, "That's not so much to ask." He looked clumsy and savage with brooding anger.

"It isn't," she said. "It isn't. God damn it, it's just not fair!" She thrust her hair back from her face with an angry swipe of her hand. He was watching her gravely, even tenderly. She whispered, "Oh, Mitch."

That was when Floyd's Oldsmobile wheeled into the street, trailing dust. Billie Jean and Theodore gathered at the barn door with Georgie, who came along dreamy-eyed, not too steady on his feet. Billie Jean kept carping like a magpie until Theodore slapped her on the rump and barked at her. Floyd drove into the barn, leaving a hazy pall in the air. Terry watched them all the way she would have watched a circling school of barracuda. Mitch slowly got to his feet and stood above her protectively;

‖ 93

he was trying to smile. She felt distantly grateful, slightly warmed; it only lasted an instant. Fear had kept coming all day in waves, at intervals she could never anticipate; now it welled up like bile in her throat. She had difficulty breathing, difficulty keeping her eyes in focus, and there was a taste on her tongue like dry brass.

Floyd appeared in the barn door with an armload of equipment that looked like a telephone repairman's gear. He was smiling coolly. He walked forward with a springy, cocky stride. The others trailed him toward the porch. He climbed up and stood two paces from her, vibrating like a time bomb; he watched Georgie stumble up into the shade and then he wheeled and grabbed the front of Mitch's shirt in his fist and dragged Mitch up on his toes. Floyd's eyes glittered frostily. He said in a very gentle voice, "Who gave him the stuff?"

"What?"

"Georgie's had his fingers in the cookie jar."

Mitch's glance whipped around toward Georgie, who stood gaunt and oblivious and smiling oafishly. "I told Theodore to watch him."

"I don't like excuses, Mitch. I can tolerate mistakes, but not excuses."

"He's *your* brother. You take care of him. I'm not his keeper."

Floyd still had Mitch's shirt bunched in his fist; he seemed indifferent to the effort it required to hold Mitch off the floor. Mitch colored and batted his arm up against Floyd's arm; Floyd let him go with a gesture of contempt. "You're forgetting, my fine buffoon, who owns the air you breathe. I can cut it off—any time."

"Go ahead, then," Mitch said bitterly. Terry backed up until her shoulders were pressed against the wall.

Georgie snuffled nervously and darted inside. Theodore stood behind Floyd, leering at Terry with his ugly eye until Floyd said over his shoulder, "Get in there and watch him. And this time do it right."

Theodore, with a low growl, turned inside. Floyd stepped aside to let Billie Jean pass but instead of following them in he stopped to rest his frightening eyes on Terry. "You won't have too much longer to wait, Sweetness."

"You talked to my father?" Her voice sounded like a stranger's.

"*Mais certainment.* He'll make the drop in the morning. After that you can go home. How does that sound?"

She shook her head, mute, distrusting. She didn't believe him for a moment. They had treated her too casually, keeping no secrets from her; a part of her mind knew they wouldn't let her go free—and another part refused to believe that, either. She felt chilled and dismal.

Floyd said casually, "Funny thing. Your daddy was pretty tough on the phone—almost as if his interest was less passionate than pecuniary. I almost had the feeling he'd rather part with you than the half million dollars."

He smiled, and after a beat he added, "But he'll go through with it." And went inside lugging his lineman's gear.

A cold knot tightened inside her. Floyd's words echoed—she almost wanted them to kill her. It would punish her father—the only kind of punishment he would understand.

Mitch stirred and said to her in his soft kind voice, "Maybe you'll get out of this yet."

She was no longer certain she wanted to.

CHAPTER Ten

Carl Oakley turned the playback switch and settled back in Earle's chair to listen to the tape for the fourth time. In the background he heard Orozco's muffled voice, talking into the phone. Frankie Adams sat at the back of the room and cleared his throat, hoarse from the fifty cigarettes he had consumed in the last eight hours.

The tape replayed the click of the telephone and the voice —uncannily Earle Conniston's voice: "Yes?"

"Conniston?"

"Yes."

"You know who this is."

"Yes."

"Okay. Hang on a minute."

The scratch of a small speaker held near the phone; Terry's voice then, difficult to make out but identifiable: "Daddy? They told me to answer the questions about what I said when you showed me the new pool and what you usually call me—I said, 'I see you've stocked it for me,' and you call me 'Baby' even though I've asked you not to. They told me to say they haven't hurt me and it's true, they haven't, but it's dark and just *miserable* and please get me out of here. They don't——"

The tape-machine was heard to click off; the kidnaper's voice said calmly, "You don't need to hear the rest of it. It satisfy you she's alive?"

"Only satisfies me she was alive when you made tape," the Conniston voice snapped. "Listen to me. Are you aware I'm very rich man? If——"

"I'm very much aware of that, Mr. Conniston." The chuckling insinuation was infuriating; listening to it for the fourth time, Oakley still found himself snarling.

The Conniston voice—Adams—went on harshly: "I'm prepared to spend every last penny to track you down, see you pay for this. Won't matter where you go, what you do. My people will find you. No trial, no do-gooder judge. Just you and me—I'll see you die as slowly and painfully as it can be done."

"Sure, Mr. Conniston. But that won't change anything. You pay up and we turn her loose. Otherwise you can kiss her off. Have you got the money?"

There was a pause; it made Oakley smile grimly. Adams had played it just right. He gave it just enough time and then said, with the proper grudging surrender in his baritone, "Yes. Unmarked small bills."

"That's just dandy. Now I'll tell you what you do with it. You pack it up in a small old suitcase—the nondescript kind that won't attract attention in a bus station. No five-hundred-dollar Vuitton luggage, understand? Borrow it from somebody in the bunkhouse if you have to. Tomorrow morning at six you get in your car and put the suitcase on the seat beside you and drive out to the state highway. Drive down through Sonoita and take the back road past Elgin and Canelo, up to Patagonia. Take the dirt road south from Patagonia toward Harshaw and Washington Camp. You know where that is?"

"I've been there a few times."

"Good. When you get past Harshaw you slow down to fifteen miles an hour and hold that speed all the way to Washington Camp. You'll have your right-hand window rolled down and the suitcase handy on the seat beside you and when you see a mirror flashing sunlight in your eyes from the trees at the side of the road you'll toss the suitcase out. Don't slow down or stop. Don't speed up. Just keep going down the road at the same speed until you get through Washington Camp. A mile or two the other side of Washington Camp you'll come to a state picnic ground at the side of the road. There may be people picnicking there and there may not be. Either way, pull into the picnic ground and sit in the car until somebody contacts you. It will either be Terry or somebody who'll tell you where to find her. Now, here's the important thing. Time your arrival so that you leave Harshaw on the road to Washington Camp at exactly seven thirty, on the button. If you reach Harshaw early wait there till seven thirty and then start, and keep a steady fifteen miles an hour all the way to the picnic ground. That'll get you to the picnic ground just before eight o'clock. Have you got it?"

"Yes."

"What kind of car will you be driving?"

"White Cadillac two-door."

"What year model?"

"This year."

"Okay. If anybody's in the car with you or we spot any official cars or airplanes or choppers you can forget all about Terry."

"Understood. I haven't informed police."

"Smart."

Beyond the kidnaper's voice Oakley heard the faint rushing woosh of a jet plane going by, on the tape—a sound like ripping cloth. The kidnaper said, "You may have to wait a little while at the picnic ground. Don't get nervous. We'll check out the money and if it's okay a signal will be passed and somebody will make contact with you. Allow at least two hours before you hit the ceiling. You'll get your daughter back if you keep your head."

Click.

Oakley switched the machine off and looked up. Orozco stood by the end of the desk, looming, a big loose brown man who sagged front and back.

Oakley said, "What about the trace?"

"They're still working on it."

"It's taking them long enough."

"I was fixin' to call back and find out," Orozco said. "There's something funny about it, though."

"What's that?"

"There's no pay phones on this local circuit. And what kind of kidnaper would use a private phone?"

"It could have been long distance. Direct-dial from a pay phone."

"You'd have heard the coins drop and the operator give him the toll charges."

Oakley scowled at him. "That's so. What are you getting at?"

"I dunno," Orozco said. "But it's funny, that's all."

Oakley reached for the glass by the phone and sipped. Earle's whiskey was a hundred proof, nine years in bond. He sat back and stuck one of Earle's H. Upmann cigars in the corner of his mouth and said disagreeably, "I don't like the feel of this. He didn't seem to care whether we traced the call or not. He stayed on that phone a hell of a long time and he never even bothered to warn us not to trace it."

"Yeah." Orozco's big fleshy face was thoughtfully creased. "Yeah. Listen, maybe——"

The phone rang. Oakley made a grab for it and barked into it; afterward his expression changed and he handed the receiver to Orozco. Orozco lifted it to his ear and talked and listened. When he hung up he said, "There wasn't any phone call."

"What?"

"No record of a call to this number on the computer."

"They're nuts. These God damned incompetent computers——"

'No. Wait a minute, Carl. Suppose it came from a wiretap."

"A what?"

"A phone they hooked up to the wire someplace. Usually when you tap a wire you just connect an earphone because you don't want to talk, you just want to listen in. But it's easy enough to connect a two-way phone to a line anyplace along the wire. Linemen do it all the time when they repair a break and then call in to the central office to check out the line. You can call any number from a lineman's phone but it doesn't get recorded on the computer because the lineman doesn't have a phone number. Get it?"

From the back of the room Frankie Adams said dryly, "That's great. You've made a discovery that deserves three Eurekas and an Edison light bulb. Now all you need to do is follow every phone wire in the southwest from one end to the other until you find one that's got holes in the insulation where they spliced into it. Give that man a great big hand, folks."

Without dignifying Adams' raucous commentary by replying, Orozco rewound the tape and switched it on again. He said, "What time did the call come in?"

"Twelve thirty-eight," Oakley said. "I wrote it down."

The tape scratched. "Yes?" "Conniston?" "Yes." "You know who this is?" It droned on. Orozco was holding his wrist as if taking his own pulse, his stare fixed on his watch. No one stirred until, near the end of the recorded dialogue, Orozco let go of his wrist and turned off the recorder. "Six minutes. That means it went over about twelve forty-four."

Oakley's eyes widened; he said softly, "Sure. The jet."

Adams complained, "What the hell are you talkin' about now?"

"Of course," Orozco observed, "it might have been a private jet or a commercial air liner, but probably it was one of them Air Force trainers from Davis Monthan up at Tucson. I don't expect they'd give out flight-plan information to just anybody but I know somebody on the Tucson police force that owes me a favor. They'll give the information to him."

"Then get at it," Oakley said. His glass was empty; he went out into the corridor. Frankie Adams trailed him to the bar. "How about explaining it to me?"

"Easy. A jet plane flew over the kidnaper at just about exactly twelve forty-four. If we can find out what planes were in the air at that time and precisely where they were, we've narrowed down the place where the phone call came from."

"That's a pretty flimsy clue."

"It's the only one we've got. When all you've got is a long shot, you shoot it."

"How about putting men on that road where they want you to make the ransom drop?"

Oakley poured a drink and said, "And suppose they were spotted?"

"Use a plane, then. A helicopter. A balloon. Hell, it shouldn't be too hard."

"Why do you think they picked that particular road? It's a

narrow dirt road that snakes through the woods like a slalom course. You can't spot it from overhead at all—the trees mask it out. And you'd have to post an army in the woods if you wanted to cover the whole road from the ground—there isn't a straight stretch of more than a hundred yards anywhere along it. It's up and down through canyons and hills all the way."

"You've got to give them credit," Adams said.

Oakley grunted and carried his drink back to the office. Orozco said, "They'll call back. I just talked to a guy in Nogales about a suitcase."

"Why go that far? We can use one of our own."

"Sometimes this new electronic stuff comes in handy. It won't hurt to have a bleeper in the suitcase."

"Bleeper?"

Orozco grinned without mirth. "One of them Mission Impossible gadgets. Small enough so you can hide it in the hinges of the suitcase. It gives off a radio signal. You use a direction-finder to pick up the signal, and you can keep tabs on the suitcase. After we get Terry back we can maybe catch up with them by radio."

"It's worth a try. But whoever they are these characters seem pretty hip."

"Sure. They may ditch the suitcase first thing. But I figure to take the chance. Can't lose much except the price of the gadget. It'll get here tonight. I told him to get a move on."

The phone rang; Orozco answered it. The conversation was brief. When he hung up he said gloomily, "Focking Air Force."

"They won't disclose the flight plans," Oakley said.

"It's classified information," Orozco said with a straight face. "Nobody knows where their planes are except them. And of course anybody who happens to be looking up at the time when they fly over. Security, you know?" He shook his head in dumbfounded exasperation. "Shit. If we had more clout we could probably force it out of them but we can't push it too hard unless we let them know what's happening."

"Which we can't do."

"Earle Conniston picked a fine time to die," Orozco agreed.

"I know a general or two in Washington. Maybe I can exercise some leverage." Oakley sat down at the phone and began to make calls. It took him twenty minutes, at the end of which time he sat back in disgust. "They're both gone for the day. They'll call back in the morning."

"Long time to wait," Orozco said.

Adams, in the doorway, said uncertainly, "On the tape he played over the phone. Terry complained about how it was dark and miserable. Dark, she said. You think that means she's blind-folded?"

"I hope to God it does," Oakley murmured. Unsatisfied, Adams drifted out of the room, his thin nostrils dilating, his fists contracting.

Oakley got up and stared out the window at a seventy-dollar cow wandering past the corral fence. Behind him Orozco said, "With Conniston dead, what's going to happen about the *chicano* land claims?"

"I wouldn't know," Oakley said absently.

"They ain't going to give up their demands just because he's dead. In fact, time his will comes up for probate, they may just challenge the whole thing in court."

"Let them. It's not my problem."

"You're the executor, ain't you?"

Oakley turned with a snap of his shoulders; irritable, he said, "Leave it be, Diego. Let's get this thing ended first."

Under the padding of flesh Orozco's blunt jaw was set. "There's people starving, Carl."

"They'll just have to go on starving until we get Terry back."

"And suppose we don't get her back? Alive, I mean."

"I told you. We'll discuss it afterwards. Now drop it."

Orozco's shrewd eyes studied him. "Okay, Carl," he murmured. "We'll talk about it tomorrow."

CHAPTER **Eleven**

The slow sleepless night spread acid through Mitch Baird; it ate away his dwindling hopes. His nerves, drawn fine, twanged with vibration. The lamp flickered on low oil; darkness condensed from the amorphous shadows like wolves.

By the back wall Theodore stood looking down intently at Billie Jean. He had a rubbery leer. They had spent half the night outside somewhere together; incessant sex was to them what opiates were to Georgie. Lamplight shone faintly on the surface of Theodore's half-closed trachomic eye.

They were all on edge. Mitch sat near the girl Terry and wondered in a dulled hopeless way what would come of her, and of himself. She had retracted into her defensive armor; she lay on her side against a rolled-up sleeping bag, her legs stretched out, picking at splinters in the floorboards with sick concentration. Staring at the lovely symmetry of her legs, Mitch imagined her—naked, pink, tender. Protective fantasies drifted in his mind, carrying him on vague sunny flights of dreams in which he vanquished all the others single-handed and spirited Terry away and was rewarded by Earle Conniston's generosity and Terry's passionate love.

He felt weight behind him and twisted his head back to see Georgie edging toward the door. Floyd, sitting by the lamp packing things away in knapsacks, said, "Where do you think you're going?"

"Bathroom."

"You just went half an hour ago."

"I can't help it," Georgie whined. "Maybe I got a bug or something."

"Have you got diarrhea?"

"Uh—a little, yeah."

Floyd watched him with a poker stare; finally he said, "All right." He cupped his hand over the lamp chimney and blew it out.

Mitch tensed in the sudden darkness. He heard Billie Jean chortle. The door was a brief pale rectangle; it closed and Floyd put a match to the lamp. Mitch glanced at Terry—still picking at splinters, indifferent to her surroundings—and went over to Floyd; he squatted down and said softly, "What happens in the morning?"

"I already explained it once. Do you need a blueprint?"

"I don't mean about the ransom. I mean about Terry."

"Indeed?"

"She gets away in one piece. We agreed on that."

"That's your problem, old cock. I wash my hands of it. Why don't you discuss it with Theodore?"

"Look, at least let me have the gun when you leave."

"Maybe. We'll see when the time comes."

Mitch tightened his stomach muscles. "How do we know you won't just pick up the ransom by yourself and keep going with it?"

"Leaving you holding the bag," Floyd said. The idea seemed to amuse him. "Of course there's Georgie. Part of the money's for him."

Unsatisfied, Mitch brooded into the lamp flame. Footsteps thudded the porch and Floyd blew the lamp out; Georgie came in. Floyd said, "Shut that door!"

It scraped shut; a match in Floyd's fingers burst painfully before Mitch's eyes. When Georgie had settled down against the far wall Floyd said, "We'll have to have a little GI party, Mitch—police the area before we clear out. We don't want to leave anything behind. Not even a Kleenex. Am I making myself understood?"

"Yes, sure."

"You can take care of that while I'm gone picking up the spoils." Floyd smiled spuriously. "Relax, old cock. Don't take things so hard."

"Easy for you to say."

"Maybe I will let you have the gun."

Mitch glanced at him quickly. There was no figuring Floyd. But then Floyd explained, "We'll be better off all around if Theodore isn't left behind to tell all about it. After all, we can hardly expect plastic surgery to do much good for Theodore, can we?"

"So you leave me to take care of the dirty work."

"Tritely put, old cock, but reasonably accurate."

"What about Billie Jean?"

"I thought you understood." Floyd was still smiling. "I'm leaving the disposition of both ladies to you."

"You bastard."

"Am I not. An interesting dilemma, what? All your humanitarian instincts of conscience dictate that you render them no harm. Yet either one of them can make deathly trouble for you —only by killing them both can you guarantee your own freedom."

"You lied to me about that plastic surgeon."

"What gives you that idea?" Floyd shook his head gently. "I didn't lie, Mitch. It wouldn't have been as interesting."

"I don't get you."

"I hardly expected you to. But it's easy to explain. Examine my options for a moment and perhaps you'll understand."

"Go on."

Floyd spread his hands with an attitude of patronizing patience. "The one unforgivable crime is murder. I have nothing against killing in principle but I recognize, purely logically, that once having committed a murder you have forfeited all possibility of mercy or, better yet, of forgetfulness. You don't follow? I'll put it another way. Crimes of property are forgivable, particularly when perpetrated against the very rich. Crimes against the person which do not in fact result in personal harm are also forgivable, particularly something like kidnaping when the victim is released unharmed. In other words if we take the ransom and run, leaving the girl alive and free, we've done nothing more lasting than depriving a wealthy man of a sum of money which he'll hardly miss. Terry hasn't been hurt. No one has been hurt—only a few feathers have been ruffled. The police and the FBI will come swarming around, searching for us, intent on capturing us and recovering the ransom, but if they don't immediately pick up our trail—if we elude them for a reasonable period of time—then the heat will die down, the ruffled feathers will lie smooth again, and it will all be forgotten in time.

"Not so with murder. Once murder has been committed the law won't let the heat die down. The feathers will stay ruffled. You understand?"

"Sure. But I don't see what it has to do with——"

"I'll proceed. Now, in the morning I'll pick up the ransom and bring it back here to be divided. You can feel reasonably certain I'll do just that because after all, you have my own brother as a hostage, so to speak. Correct? All right. Now I've let you in on my personal plans. I intend to take my share of the ransom and one of the cars and split from here—by myself. The rest of you will be left to fend for yourselves. You will be the only one armed. You will no doubt hold the others at bay, put Terry in the sports car and drive away with her, leaving the other three stranded here on foot. That will give you ample time to drop Terry off at a safe place, and time to get yourself across the border with your share of the loot. Now we return to your original question—did I or did I not tell the truth about von Roon?"

Floyd paused and took out his wallet. From it he withdrew a dog-eared snapshot. Mitch held it close to the lamp and leaned forward to examine it. The photograph showed part of a street —half a block of single-story adobe buildings jammed together along a chuck-holed street that had no sidewalk. Centered in the picture was a building with a pale stucco front and a wooden sign fixed above the door: FARMACIA—*G. von Roon.*

Floyd said, "Keep it if you like. The town's called Caborca."

Mitch lifted his eyes from the photo to Floyd's somber dark face. "How do I know you didn't just make up the whole yarn to fit some old snapshot you happened to pick up? Maybe there *is* a guy named von Roon but how do I know he's a plastic surgeon like you said?"

Floyd opened his wallet again and took out a one-column newspaper clipping. It was yellow and brittle, ready to break at the folded seams. Mitch scanned it briefly. The article, clipped from a three-year-old *New York Times,* was an inside-page feature tracing the whereabouts of Nazi war criminals who had been released from prison after serving Nuremberg sentences. One paragraph was circled in ball-point ink:

> Gerhard von Roon, 71, was once a surgeon at the Vorbeck-berg hospital complex, where human guinea pigs suffered and died in surgical experiments. Israeli sources allege von Roon, a plastic surgeon, has disguised a score of top Nazi fugitives who have disappeared and never been brought to trial. Authorities in Mexico, where von Roon now has a pharmacy in a small village, have been unable to confirm such charges. Recently interviewed, von Roon laughed with the expansive air of a man without secrets. He said, "They suffer from paranoia. I am only a pharmacist—see for yourself." He lives quietly, seems well liked in the community of Caborca where he works, and talks freely about any subject except the Nazi years—a subject he considers closed. "I have served my sentence."

Floyd Rymer said quietly, "The point is, old cock, I was forced to tell you the truth. Otherwise if you thought you had no way out you'd most likely turn yourself in to the law. But I'm giving you a way out. A hundred thousand dollars tax-free and a new face."

"Aeah," Mitch said dully.

"It's my only guarantee you won't betray me—you see? Because if I didn't give you this choice you'd turn state's evidence and put the FBI on my tail. But even with time off you wouldn't get out in less then ten or fifteen years. This way you're free and rich. And so am I."

"And nobody gets killed?"

Floyd smiled. "Now you've got it."

It made a kind of sense. But he still didn't trust Floyd.

Floyd added, as an afterthought, "One thing, Mitch. When you dump Terry out make sure she's far enough from civilization to give you a good head start before she gets a chance to start talking. Ditch her car somewhere and buy a clean car—don't take buses or planes. Always travel by car. It's hardest for anyone to find out where you came from or where you went."

Mitch half-heard the last of it: he was looking past Floyd at the crumpled shape by the far wall. He said nervously, "What's wrong with him?"

"Who?" Floyd swiveled to look. "Georgie?" He got to his feet and raised his voice: "George!"

Georgie didn't stir. Floyd walked forward, increasing the pace as he approached; he was almost running when he reached his brother. He went down on one knee and gripped Georgie's shoulder and shook him. Georgie rolled over sluggishly, blinked and laughed. "The hell time's it?"

Floyd said without turning, "Mitch. Bring that food sack over here."

The noise had roused the others. Terry was sitting up, looking back and forth, puzzled; the two in the back corner came forward into the lamplight and watched. Mitch took the knapsack over to Floyd and watched him paw through it. Floyd dumped everything out, opened a cracker tin and drew several packets from it. His eyes counted them; he tossed them aside and said something in his throat. Mitch couldn't make out the words.

Floyd's head skewed back. "Well?" he demanded.

"Well what? I didn't hear what you said."

Georgie mumbled, "The hell time's it?"

Mitch said uncertainly, "He's freaked out."

Georgie cackled. His mouth worked and after a moment he said in a slurred breathless whisper, "Man, blowin' my—mind!" He simpered and crawled around on the floor, rolling up in a fetal ball. The pupils of his eyes were pinpoints; the irises around them seemed enlarged with bloodshot veins. He was having a great deal of trouble getting his breath.

Floyd said lamely, "Take it easy—take it easy."

Georgie made no response. His eyes turned dull like slate; they closed. He lay curled up, wheezing.

Mitch said, "What's the matter with him?"

Floyd didn't answer for the longest time. Mitch felt a hand on his arm—Terry, clutching him for strength. Billie Jean and Theodore hung back at the edge of the shadows, watching, afraid to speak. Afterward, remembering it, Mitch wondered how it was that they had all *known*, before anyone had said much of anything at all.

Finally Floyd said without tone, "I think he's had it—I think he's had it."

Mitch felt his muscles go rigid. He cleared his throat. Floyd seemed to think the sound was a question. He said, "Overdose of heroin depresses the respiratory system. Slows down all the vital functions. He's got congestion in his lungs now—I think he's had it."

None of them moved. Floyd said, "You may leave me alone now. All of you." When he looked up his expression was astringent, unforgiving. It lay against Theodore and then it came around against Mitch like a bladed weapon. Mitch backed up, dragging Terry with him. The four of them retreated beyond the lamp and stood in a loose knot. None of them said anything. From where he stood, Mitch saw Georgie's face change. Georgie began to frown like a small child sleeping—solemn, innocent. The sound of his labored wheezing became louder and slower in the silent dim store.

Georgie must have found the heroin in the cracker tin when Theodore left him alone inside; Georgie's trips to the bathroom had given him the time to mainline the stuff. He had injected too many shots in too short a time—that was all.

Mitch felt Terry's fingers crawl up his arm and clamp onto his shoulder. She turned her face against his chest. He slipped his arm around her and gripped her waist. She stopped shaking and stood rigid, waiting. The only sound was the rattle of Georgie's breath. It became raspy and irregular; the intervals of silence grew longer. All the while, Floyd squatted on his heels with one hand on Georgie's neck, not blinking, not stirring. Georgie's skin turned gray and grainy like a matte finish. Hunched over him, Floyd resembled a pagan priest entranced in some macabre rite. It was as if he intended the power of life to flow through the tips of his fingers, lightly resting on the side of Georgie's neck, to resurrect the dying: as if by the sheer force of mental concentration he could will life into Georgie.

A time came when Mitch took a deep breath and realized he had himself stopped breathing; it had been a long time since he had last breathed; he panted to get air in his lungs—and realized in that moment that he had begun to hold his breath when Georgie had stopped gasping.

Floyd stood up briskly and turned. His face was composed: his expression like a natural law left nothing open to dispute. "Strip off his clothes—don't forget his watch and ring. Dump him out in the desert."

Billie Jean said, "You mean bury him?"

"No." Moving like a mechanism, Floyd walked to the back of the room and sat down in the debris with his back against the wall. "No. Leave him out there naked where the coyotes and buzzards can get at his face. The ants will finish the job." Momentarily his eyes flashed: "Or do you want the cops to identify him and track us all down through him?"

Terry shuddered violently. Her little cries were muffled against Mitch's chest. He tightened his grip and muttered, "You do it, Theodore."

Theodore glanced at him, lugubrious; if Theodore had any feelings about it he did not display them. He went slowly toward Georgie and bent down and Mitch turned away, unable to watch; he cupped his hand at the back of Terry's head to keep her face against his chest. Floyd, sitting with his knees drawn up, lowered his face and closed his eyes. Billie Jean began to whimper.

Floyd never glanced at any of them after that. Theodore went out, carrying Georgie. Billie Jean lit a stick of pot and even offered it around but no one wanted it and Billie Jean settled down in a corner, hunched around her smoke, taking quick little furtive puffs. Mitch held Terry close to him until she stopped trembling, whereupon she turned away from him and settled to the floor much the way a pneumatic tire settles when punctured. She watched Floyd the way she might have watched a clock ticking toward—what? Mitch kept his uneasy stare on her; he pressed his hands together until he heard the knuckles crack.

Withdrawn and brooding, Floyd sat surrounded by a coiling charge of electric malevolence which tightened notch by notch as the night passed. His immobile silence was more sinister than a furious rage.

When Theodore returned he dropped Georgie's clothes in a bundle on the floor and obliviously opened a can of beer and drank it quickly, afterward belching with loud satisfaction. So far as Mitch could tell Floyd didn't even glance at him. In her corner Billie Jean mewed like a frightened kitten but Theodore only turned his head to stare at her; he did not go to her. They all remained like that, squatting in their individual solitary caves of silence across a lengthening stretch of time which to Mitch seemed almost visible, like a sheet of glass slowly disintegrating into brittle frosty fragments.

Mitch waited through the awful stillness without reckoning the passage of hours. A point came when he found himself sitting crosslegged, his hand on the silken warmth of Terry Conniston's forearm, her head propped gently against his shoulder—he did not remember moving to her, nor remember her responding to his intrusion. Her eyes had gone dark behind their opaque placenta of fear; he understood that she was clinging to him only because it was better than sitting alone, untouched, in taut terrible emptiness.

She seemed unaware of the fact that he was looking at her, or perhaps indifferent to it. Her lower lip jutted in profile—afraid, defiant, infuriated by her own despair. The bare triangle of smooth golden skin at her throat held his attention: the round thrusting solidity of her breasts, the concave crescent of her narrow waist, the round line of strong hip and long flank outlined against the dying lamp, and on her face the traces, etching deeper, of heavy and desperate strain.

The lamp went dry and the flame flickered out and it slowly penetrated Mitch's dulled consciousness that streaks of gray light were sharding in through cracks around the windows and door. He got up, stiff in all his joints, slipping Terry's hand out of his grip, and crossed to the front of the place. When he dragged the door open it squealed and scratched its way across an arc of sand and pebbles on the floor. The indeterminate half-light of dawn sprawled in through the opening, throwing a vague splash across the floor toward the spot where Georgie had died. Mitch stood in the open rectangle breathing the crisp air, pushing the residue of stale pot smoke from his nostrils.

When he turned back inside the light was growing stronger; Floyd's eyes lay against him like glass-cutting diamonds, motionless but ready to slice. Mitch stood bolt still in his tracks.

Floyd was getting to his feet. Straightening up, looking at each of them in turn, walking slowly forward trailing uncertain mystery like a cloak: he passed Mitch a foot away and went on out through the door, ducking his head beneath the tilted beam.

Mitch waited ten seconds; then his eyes grew wide and he wheeled under the beam, outside.

Floyd stood out in the street, ten feet from the porch, frowning thoughtfully at the eastern sky. Half the sun was a red ball on a mountaintop. Floyd seemed to have the peripheral vision of a professional basketball player: he swiveled his head to look at Mitch, who had taken one step onto the porch and was standing still in deep shadows. The adrenaline pumping through his body made Mitch's hands shake.

Floyd bent down slowly and picked up a clot of clay the size of his thumb. He rubbed it between his fingers until it disintegrated in a little shower of sand. Turning his face toward Mitch, he spoke from his semi-crouch:

"About that time."

Floyd's eyes seemed voracious. He put his right hand in the slit pocket of his jacket—the pocket where he kept the revolver. Mitch did not stir; he only breathed again when Floyd turned with a sharp snap of his shoulders and stalked across the street toward the barn.

The Oldsmobile started up and came out of the barn slowly, crunching stones. It stopped below the porch and Floyd leaned across to the open right-hand window. "Enjoy yourself," he said, and tossed the revolver to the ground below the porch.

Mitch glimpsed Floyd's hot quick smile and then the Oldsmobile's engine roared. The tires spun, spraying back salvos, then gained purchase. The big car surged away, covering Mitch with dust.

He stepped down off the porch and picked up the gun. It occurred to him then that Floyd's own emotions were no more important to Floyd than his tonsils, which had been removed in his childhood. Nothing would distract Floyd from his logically constructed plans.

Mitch had not known what to expect; frozen with fear, he had half believed Floyd would explode against them all. Now his brain slowly clamped onto the new realization after numbly dislodging from its former suspicion. Floyd meant to go through with it all as if nothing had happened.

The weight of the gun was unfamiliar in his hand. He turned and saw Theodore and Billie Jean standing just outside the door.

Billie Jean said matter-of-factly. "I don't think he's gonna come back."

Theodore sat down with his legs dangling over, gripped the edge of the porch with both hands and rocked back and forth. The milky half-closed eye caught a glint of sunlight; he said, "You got the gun, Mitch. You want to do it or do I?"

"Do what?"

Theodore shrugged and kept rocking. "Her," he said.

"Nobody's touching her," Mitch said. Rage swelled his eyes, fueled and banked by the long repressed night.

Billie Jean said, "She knows what we look like."

Mitch didn't reply. Theodore fixed his one-eyed stare on the gun and stopped rocking; his legs became still. Billie Jean said, "When Floyd gets back we ain't going to want to waste a lot of time. Better get done with it now."

"You just said you thought he wasn't coming back. Make up your mind."

"Either way," Billie Jean said, "we got to stop her clock, don't we? I mean, we can't take her with us and we can't leave her here to talk."

"We'll wait for Floyd," Mitch said.

Theodore said, "Georgie's dead. What's he got to come back here for?"

The edge of that thought, fast-traveling, struck them all a

sharp blow. Mitch's eyes widened; he said, "We wait," with more confidence than he felt.

Billie Jean said crossly, "He owes us money."

"You're talking as if he'd already run out on us."

"Well, he has. You know he has. Who's going to stop him pick up the money and just keep going across the line? Was you him, would *you* come back?"

I would, Mitch thought. *But I'm not him. He wouldn't be afraid of the rest of us coming after him.*

As if reading his thoughts Billie Jean said, "Suppose'n he picks up the money and then he stops at a phone and tells the cops where to look for us."

Theodore scowled. "Floyd wouldn't do that to us."

"You wanna *bet?*"

Terry Conniston appeared in the door, pale and unsteady; clearly she had been listening. She fastened her gaze on Mitch. Theodore's head twisted around on his short neck; he said in his casual abrasive voice, "We oughta use that gun on her now and get out of here, go on down the road and watch for Floyd. If Floyd comes, okay. If the cops come we fade back in the rocks and let them go by and then get the hell out of there. There's a good spot up the road ten–twelve miles from here."

Billie Jean said with waspish petulance, "We ain't got any more time to wait."

Mitch shook his head obstinately. "Anyway the car's only a two-seater. And Floyd's got the keys to it."

"You wanna get us all put away?"

"We wait," Mitch said, and set his teeth.

Theodore growled. He turned around again to fix his cyclopean stare on Terry, who shrank back in the doorway and gripped the jamb, the tendons of her fingers standing out. Billie Jean lowered her brows and walked to the edge of the porch, sat down beside Theodore and bent to whisper in his ear. Mitch frowned and took a step forward. Theodore's eye whipped around toward him and Theodore nodded in response to something Billie Jean said. Billie Jean formed her hand into a fist and pounded her knee, talking with sibilant earnestness; Mitch, unable to make out the words, kept walking forward.

He came within six feet of them: Billie Jean stopped whispering, gave him an arch look and stood up. Mitch pointed the gun at them. "You two gentle down."

Billie Jean started to walk back along the porch toward the door. "You figure just wait here till the cops come, Mitch? What do you hear from your head lately?"

She stopped at the door. Her plump face was turned toward Mitch—but her hand darted out, clamped around Terry's wrist and yanked Terry out onto the porch. Terry's little cry brought Mitch up on the porch; he extended the gun before him and said, "Let her go!"

Billie Jean's sensuous mouth formed a pouting leer. Terry grabbed her hand and tried to pry it loose. Mitch took another step toward them—and Theodore landed on him like a cement bag.

They had set it up between them—Billie Jean's distraction, Theodore's leap: he had fallen for it like an idiot. He had time for that disgusted thought in the instant when he felt the rush of wind from Theodore's charging attack. Then he was pitching forward, agony exploding in his back where Theodore's knee had rammed him; spinning, his wrist caught in Theodore's fist. He went down with Theodore on top of him and the gun fell somewhere. The tumble, and Theodore's weight, knocked the wind out of his lungs; a curse, savage but weak, escaped his mouth. Theodore grunted and twisted something and Mitch's face was pushed down against the splintered porch boards. He felt something rip along the side of his jaw; only then did he begin to react. He was not a fighter but there was enough screaming panic in him to inject strength: he flailed his body, striking back with both heels, and hit some part of Theodore, enough to make Theodore shift his weight and cry out. Mitch got one elbow under him and heaved, rolling them both over. Theodore switched his grip from Mitch's wrist to his torso and pinned one arm against his side in a cruel hug. Nothing was in focus or balance; Mitch couldn't see through the red wash of outrage and terrified frustration that filled his eyes. Agony pulled at his mouth. Kicking blindly, he got purchase against a post and heaved again. It threw him off the porch. There was a sickening instant in mid-air, rolling over, like a dream of falling. They spun together and hit the dusty earth with a whacking thud. Somehow Mitch was on top of Theodore. The fall broke Theodore's grip and Mitch felt himself rolling free. Stunned and spastic, he whipped around on hands and knees, scrabbling to get his feet under him.

He brought things into focus and saw several things at once. On the porch both girls were diving toward the fallen gun. On the ground before him Theodore was rolling toward the kitchen knife which must have fallen out of Mitch's belt.

Mitch felt needles in his legs. With a cry he launched himself forward: he brought his hand up with deathly panic behind it, whacking the heel of his hand up under Theodore's nose. It lifted Theodore off the ground: he heard the crush of cartilage, felt the spurt of blood on his palm; Theodore windmilled, off balance, and slammed his back against the edge of the porch. Behind Theodore the girls were a blur of swirling flesh, a cacophony of shrieks.

Theodore roared and bounced forward, his eye glittering. Light raced along the blade of the knife in his sweeping fist. Horror froze a knot in Mitch's throat. He tried to dodge and his heel slipped on the loose pebbles of the street and as he fell his right leg whipped out for balance. Theodore tripped over it and sprawled, still roaring. Mitch reached for the edge of the porch to lift himself to his feet; as he got to his knees he saw, at eye-level, the revolver come skittering across the boards— kicked by one of the girls' thrashing feet.

Unwilled, automatically, his fist closed around the gun and he wheeled in time to see Theodore rushing toward him with the knife outstretched at groin level, ready to rip him up the belly. In unthinking reaction Mitch yanked the gun around and jerked the trigger, and kept jerking the trigger with deliberate, methodical, mechanical pulls.

The gunshots were earsplitting roars; the bullets sprayed out, making the gun pitch and buck in his fist; more than one of them, fired point-blank, struck Theodore. Red spots started to show up on his shirt even before he stopped moving. A dark disk appeared on his face just above his bad eye, rimmed at the bottom by droplets of crimson froth. In slack-mouthed disbelief Mitch watched him turn aside like a puppet and take a dozen jerky disjointed steps and topple—dead, clearly, by the way he fell.

The firecracker scent of cordite was a vicious bite in Mitch's nostrils. Blood dripped from the scraped side of his jaw. He had a stitch in his ribs; he stood soaked in his own juices, staring down at the trail of blood spots that marked Theodore's last few steps.

Dull amazement washed through him; he was not ready to credit the reality of it. It was only after some time that he thought to turn around—he almost lost his balance—toward the porch where the girls had been struggling.

They stood a little distance apart, staring. The gunshots must have broken up their fight. Terry slowly sat down and buried her face in her hands; her body lurched but she made no sounds. Billie Jean waited a long time before she climbed down off the porch and walked past Mitch as if he weren't there and stood over Theodore's crumpled body. She prodded Theodore with her toe. There was a reflexive muscle-jerk that made Theodore's leg clatter; Billie Jean jumped back in terror. Mitch bent down by her and felt for a pulse but he wasn't sure where to look: he tried the wrist and the throat. He peeled back the lid of Theodore's good eye but blood filled it immediately; he wiped his hand on the sandy ground and backed away, and ran to the corner of the barn, where he bent over and threw up.

He was a long time sick. Finally he wiped his mouth furiously on a handkerchief and came back across the street, taking a long detour to avoid going near Theodore. Billie Jean was crouching below the porch, watching Theodore anxiously as if she was waiting for him to get up.

Full of fury Mitch kicked her in the thigh and when she looked up he said, "It's your fault! You killed him!" His voice trembled.

Billie Jean looked at him with a slowly changing face; with childish petulance she said, finally, "Bullshit."

He looked past her, up across the porch. Terry looked bleak and glazed. He climbed up and went over to her and sat down beside her. She didn't say anything; she didn't even look at him. There was a long livid scratch down her cheek and her clothing was torn, her hair a matted tangle. She was sucking on a broken fingernail.

At the edge of the porch Billie Jean got up, rising into sight like a porpoise coming up from the sea. She said in a practical voice, "Let's don't just leave him out there in the middle of the street like that."

Mitch thought about it sluggishly. "Do what you want to do."

"I can't move him by myself. He weighs too much."

Unreasonable and loud, he shouted, "What the hell do you want me to do? Bury him with full military honors? Embalm him and build a thousand-dollar casket? Leave me alone!"

Very businesslike, Billie Jean only waited out his tirade patiently and then said, "Do the same thing he did with Georgie."

Mitch resisted it for half an hour but in the end he did what Billie Jean wanted because it was the only thing he could do. He didn't know where Theodore had put Georgie and he didn't want to find out. He put Theodore around back of the store near an anthill and left him there bloody and naked. He carried Theodore's clothes inside and stuffed them into a knapsack with Georgie's things. Working mindlessly, doing what Floyd had ordered last night, he policed the place, picked up every last scrap and carried everything across the street into the barn. The trunk of the sports car was not locked; he put everything into it and had to sit on the lid to close it.

He stood in the barn entrance, soaked in sweat and caked with dirt and blood. He felt feverish, drugged. Across the powder-stripe between the buildings Terry Conniston was standing near the place where Theodore had died. She had picked up the knife. Billie Jean slumped resentfully against the edge of the porch, breathing hard, her big breasts rising and falling. Evidently they had both thought of the knife at the same time and Terry had won the race for it.

Mitch still had the gun in his hip pocket. He took it out and after a minute discovered how to break the cylinder open. All the cartridges had been fired. He put it back in his pocket and started to cross the street.

Billie Jean said, "Well?"

"Well what?" he snapped.

"What do we do now?"

"Christ, how the hell should I know?"

"You better think of something," Billie Jean said. "I don't think Floyd's gonna come back." By some simple animalistic process she had already put Theodore completely out of her thoughts. She said again, matter-of-fact, "He ain't coming back. You know he ain't."

CHAPTER **Twelve**

Carl Oakley sat in the Cadillac behind rolled-up tinted windows, wearing a hat and dark glasses and hoping he looked enough like Earle Conniston from a distance to pass the test. He twisted in his seat to sweep the picnic area and the cottonwood–sycamore copse that surrounded it; nothing stirred except a few birds and a few leaves, roughed up by the wind. He looked at his watch, because the dashboard clock like all dashboard clocks did not work—almost three hours since he had arrived. The engine had begun to overheat and he had switched it off, killing the air-conditioner; he had started it up at fifteen-minute intervals to cool down the interior. In these hills the heat wasn't too bad but he was covered with a nervous glaze of oil-sweat.

He chewed a cigar and felt an acid pain in his gut—the sense that it was already too late. They had likely murdered Terry long since: he ought to call in the police. But the police would insist on talking to Earle.

Forty-eight hours ago Oakley had considered himself an honest man, within the acknowledged flexibility of business morals. He was surprised by the ease with which he had shattered that illusion. What he was doing was illegal, dangerous, and inexcusably dishonest, and during the night he had traveled the full length of rationalizations and faced the reality of his crime. All these years he had enjoyed the self-satisfied comfort of the knowledge that he did not covet what was not rightfully his. To the best of his belief he had never envied Earle Conniston, never resented the difference in their stations nor been tempted to cheat Earle—a temptation which, had it existed, would not have been difficult to fulfill. Earle had trusted him with unreserved confidence; Oakley had enjoyed the smug satisfaction of knowing Earle's confidence was deserved. Today, in hindsight, he marveled at his own record of pious self-righteousness.

The new ambitiousness could not have sprung full-blown into his consciousness like a fully shaped god from the head of Zeus; it must have been there all the time, undetected, waiting. What had triggered it had been the sudden awareness that Earle was shrinking—no longer the larger-than-life idol who had moved through the corporate world with demoniacal grace, pokerish imperterbability, uncanny judgment, athletic balance. Not until Earle had revealed unmistakably his own weakness had insidious thoughts wriggled past Oakley's puritan conscience, changed wish to desire; and even then, he thought, it was unlikely he'd have done anything about it if Earle had lived. The options would have been unfavorable. Petty embezzlement? Even if he had been convinced he could get away with it, it was beneath him. A full-scale raid designed to wrest the empire from Earle? No: he lacked the calculated brutality for that, the rapier fineness, the stamina, the acrobatic agility. He was a good lawyer, sensitive to subtlety and nuance, alert to opportunity, keen to the openings that were to be found between the fine-print lines of financial documentation. He had discovered, investigated, discarded and recommended countless deals for Earle Conniston; he had protected the empire against incursion and insult; he had unerringly weeded out deadwood and dispassionately called for its amputation. But he had achieved these successes because he had been confident, and he had been confident because he was backed by Earle's weight. Thinking it through relentlessly he had concluded that the lucky timing of Earle's death had been the only event in the world which could possibly have given him both the opportunity and the resolve to make his grab.

He didn't know whether to feel grateful or angry. Something Earle had said ten years ago remained in his head as if written in letters of fire: *In anything you do, risk is determined not by what you stand to win but by what you stand to lose.* Today, for the first time in his life, Oakley had committed himself fully: he stood to lose everything. Absolutely, literally everything. It frightened him.

In his way Oakley had always been a fatalist. Things were determined by chance as often as not. Luck: the very fact that he existed at all was only a matter of chance. How had his father happened to meet his mother? How had he, a bright but undistinguished young lawyer, chanced to meet Earle Conniston at precisely the opportune moment for them both? It had been, he recalled, at a poker game—the perfect setting. The shape of a man's life was carved not only by his own decisions and reactions but, equally as much, by blind coincidence, sheer accident. Luck.

It was Earle's bad luck, and perhaps Oakley's good luck, that Earle had blundered into Louise's bedroom at the wrong moment, blundered into Frankie Adams' drop-kick, blundered against the bedpost. It amazed Oakley that his conscience remained untroubled. Not responsible for Earle's death, he felt no guilt about the course he had pursued since then—unless guilt could be defined as the gnawing fear that his whole scheme would collapse, with him under it.

He inspected his watch irritably and shot his cuff. Ten past eleven. He had arrived before eight o'clock after making the ransom drop along the road as instructed. Presumably Orozco's operatives in Nogales were monitoring the radio signal from the bugged suitcase which contained the money.

He sat it out another twenty minutes, at the end of which time he got out of the car and walked around the clearing, went into the woods and scoured the ground, not sure what he was looking for but half afraid he might stumble across Terry's body. He found nothing at all to indicate the kidnapers had ever been there. He went back to the car and rolled out of the clearing with the air-conditioner roaring softly. The big car took the rutted roads fast, swaying on its springs, bottoming now and then with a sickening bang. By the time he reached Patagonia he had chewed his cigar to mangled shreds; he scraped the remains off his fingers in the dashboard ashtray and bumped across the railroad tracks and put the car onto the paved road to Sonoita, gunning it up to ninety across the rolling valley.

Shortly before one o'clock he turned in at the main gate and started up the last few miles to the house. The ranch sprawled toward the horizons—a thousand miles of fence, a hundred windmills, fifteen thousand cattle, five thousand acres of irrigated Pima cotton, two hundred cowboys and farmhands, six hundred horses and eighteen tractors, uncounted coyotes and coveys of quail. The Conniston ranch: a small corner of the empire. Carl Oakley surveyed it with a proprietary air while he tooled the car expertly toward the big house.

Orozco was waiting by the garage when he came out. Oakley said, "No sign of her. I waited three and a half hours."

"I'm sorry, Carl."

"You think she's dead, then?"

"I guess she is. But we got to keep lookin' anyway."

They walked up to the house, Orozco talking on the way: "Your buddy at the Pentagon built a fire under the dispatcher at Davis Monthan. They let us have the flight plans of the planes they had in the air yesterday and we narrowed it down to five possibilities. I got men out checking all five areas now. One of them was right over downtown Tucson, which ain't going to be much help. I told them we wanted to know where the planes were at twelve forty-four but the guy pointed out one of those jets covers maybe ten miles in one minute between twelve forty-three and a half, and twelve forty-four and a half. Not to mention if your watch was off by half a minute or two minutes."

They went inside. Louise and Adams sat gloomily at a table in the front room playing gin rummy. Oakley said, "She didn't turn up," and headed for the corridor, ignoring their questions. Orozco trailed him into the office and shut the door. Oakley said, "What about the bug in the suitcase?"

"It went over the border at Lochiel and they lost the signal."

"They *what?*" Oakley wheeled.

"Look, Carl, a little transmitter like that ain't got a whole lot of range. Maybe we'll pick it up again. I got men on every road south out of Lochiel."

"They'd damned well better find it."

"You get no guarantees in this business. We do our best."

"You sound like a God damned used-car salesman on South Sixth in Tucson."

Orozco grinned. "I used to be." He pointed a pudgy finger and, following his glance, Oakley saw a map pinned up against the bookshelves; it hadn't been there before. Orozco said, " 'Scuse me for making the place into a war room but I'm tryin' to run the whole operation by phone from here." He went over to the map and beckoned. "Look here. I got men in Nogales and Magdalena. Ain't all that many roads leading out of Lochiel— sooner or later the bleeper's got to go through somewhere around there unless they get smart and ditch it or double back this side of the border, in which case I got a man posted at Lochiel. We'll turn them up. Just a matter of time."

"Unless they stop to divide up the money and leave the suit-case on a junk heap at Cananea."

"I've got boys closing in. If it's there they'll find it."

"Sure. Then what?"

Orozco shrugged. "You got to play this kind of thing by ear, Carl."

"And what am I supposed to do in the meantime? Sit here on my ass and diddle myself?"

Orozco brought up a straight chair from the back of the room and reversed it, sitting down cowboy-fashion, astraddle with his thick arms folded across the high back of the chair. "Time we had that little talk about the ranch, Carl. I told you I'd bring it up today."

"This isn't the time for it."

"Hell it ain't. What else you got to talk about right now?"

"I don't want to talk at all."

"Too bad, because I got a few things to say."

Oakley sat back in Earle's leather chair and closed his eyes painfully. It didn't discourage Orozco; the fat man launched into a droning speech.

"In the past year Earle's had four fences pulled down and two barns burned to the ground. That's just kid stoff, sure—nothing you can't handle. But you keep turnin' a deaf ear to these *chicanos* and their *machismo* is going to cause a rising. They see black people getting concessions all over the place and they figure it's their turn, you know? If the blacks can do it so can the Mexicanos. You ever been out in the scrub behind this ranch out east, Carl? You ever visited a family of *chicanos* livin' fourteen to a three-room 'dobe hut, the house full of malnutrition and TB and unemployment and infant mortality? When they can they pick peas for a dollar a day and when they can't they live on tortillas and beans. Maybe one kid gets a job as a yard boy or carry-out boy. Sitting up there in the scrub hills lookin' down on this ranch and this big house, all of which got stolen from those people's grandparents. You know how they did that, Carl? Easy. A honnerd years ago the Mexican goes into the crossroads gringo store to buy a sack of feed and the storekeeper says, 'Sign here and I'll give you credit,' and the *chicano* goes ahead and signs a paper he can't read because he needs the credit. Turns out he's signed a deed to his land. The judges and the lawyers and the tax collectors and every gringo in Arizona defrauded these people out of their birthrights. Now they want 'em back. They want to know if you're gonna give it to them or if they're gonna have to take it."

Orozco's voice ran down; Oakley kept his eyes shut. His silence argued with Orozco.

Orozco said stubbornly, "I got a cousin out in the back hills there livin' on beans and bread. No meat, no milk. They get their drinking water from an irrigation ditch. Conniston's been gettin' farm payments from the government that exceed the income of every *chicano* in this county put together. My cousin's gettin' fed up, Carl."

Oakley opened his eyes with a grimace and studied the fat man with cool mistrust. "If he's your cousin why do you let him live like that?"

"Because he's too proud to accept my help. I've offered him money plenty times."

"But he's not too proud to demand title to land he never earned."

"That's a redneck argument, Carl. I didn' expect it from you. 'Look at the lazy greaser, good for nahthing, livin' on welfare.' Only there ain't no welfare down here to speak of. Just gringos complainin' about the lazy nogood greasers."

"Don't call me a bigot, Diego. You know damn well when I'm in trouble I'd sooner go to you for help than any gringo I know."

"Sure. And when was the last time you invited a *chicano* into your home for a nice sociable dinner?"

Oakley tipped his head back and closed his eyes down to slits. "You're way out of line, Diego. Don't start calling me names just because your *chicanos* just can't adjust to the times. How can you try to bulldoze me with a fantastic pipedream like this? Conniston Industries has firm, clear title to this ranch. This wild *chicano* talk is going to do about as much good as a girl saying she wants her virginity back." Abruptly he shot his eyes wide open and leaned forward, elbows on the desk, as if to catch Orozco off guard. "The fact of the matter is you got roped into *La Causa* by some crazy fanatic or other who knew you had a pipeline to Conniston through me and now you're going through the motions because you don't want your friends to call you a *Tio Taco* or a *vendido* or a *Malinchista* sellout Uncle Tom. All right, you made your pitch and I didn't buy it. Let's drop it, all right? Go back and tell them I'm not in the market."

"You don' think much of me, do you?"

"I think a lot of you, Diego, but I think you got yourself roped into a mistake because you didn't stop and use your head first."

"You think I'm just an errand boy for some big-shot Mexican that runs the movement, hey?" Orozco smiled slowly. "I got news for you, Carl. I *am* the movement."

Oakley scowled. "I'm not impressed. I gave you more credit for brains."

"Did you? Did I mention I'm planning to run for the state senate next year?"

"More power to you," Oakley said with distaste; he was about to add a sharp remark when the phone rang. He grabbed it spitefully. "Hello."

"Mr. Oakley, please?" A girl's flat-chested chirp.

"Speaking."

"Mr. Burns calling, sir? Of Cleland, Burns and Lee, broker-age? Hold on, please, sir?"

". . . Hello, Carl? Jim Burns here. On that short-sell order of yours, Conniston Industries common. The stock opened an eighth of a point down this morning and it's lost three eighths in the day's trading."

"What of it?" Oakley snapped.

"Well, just this. There seems to be a lot of short-selling in the stock and it's disturbed the market. I feel obliged to remind you that you can't complete a short sale unless there's been an up-tick since you placed the order. There has been no uptick. As of this afternoon's close, New York time, the stock is half a point below the point where it was when you put through the order. In good conscience I felt I'd better warn you—you could easily be caught holding the bag."

"There'll be an uptick," Oakley said curtly.

"Then you're reconfirming the order?"

"Of course I am."

"Fine—fine. It's just that I felt a duty to make sure you under-stood that——"

"I understand everything," Oakley said. "Good-bye." He dropped the receiver onto the phone with a racket and mut-tered an oath.

Orozco was watching him with guileless blandness. Oakley picked up the phone and dialed a Los Angeles number; went through a switchboard and a secretary and finally got to the man he wanted. "Phil, I want you to place an order with the floor specialist for five thousand shares of Conniston Industries. I want it done in such a way that the market is aware that I'm the one placing the order. Can do?"

"It can be done—but why? Didn't you just sell a hundred thousand shares short through our office?"

"I did. I trust you're keeping that under your hat."

"Your name hasn't been mentioned. Oh—I see. You want to force an uptick to get out from under the short sales."

"Will you do it?"

A pause; then, in a more cautious tone, "Why not? I get a commission, don't I?"

"Thank you," Oakley said. When he hung up his face was less taut.

Orozco said, "The market assumes that if a close insider like you buys a block of stock like that, it must be going up. So you get your uptick and then you announce Earle Conniston's death and the price of the stock dives to the floor and you make a few million bucks on your short sales. Cute."

"I didn't know you followed the market."

"I'd have to be pretty thick in the head not to follow what you're up to," Orozco said. "It ain't no skin off my nose, except I won't feel so bad about socking you with a king-size bill for the job I been doing here."

"I won't haggle over it," Oakley said, and exchanged a guarded glance with the fat man in which there was the gleam of shrewd mutual understanding. Oakley leaned back in the expensive leather chair and put a cigar in his mouth and smiled. It was quite some time before he realized, not without dismay, that he hadn't even thought about Terry Conniston once in the past hour.

CHAPTER **Thirteen**

Mitch's right hand was swollen; clumsy and jumpy, he had pushed the red sports car out of the barn to get more light on the work but still the shadows beneath the dash conspired against him. He lay on his back like a contortionist, both legs hanging out the open door, the small of his back painfully braced against the ridge of the doorsill. His arms, lifted above his head, kept tiring quickly and he had to lower them to his chest and rest them. He had positioned the car so that by raising his head he could look past his knees at the porch of the abandoned store across the street; thus, at quick intervals, he kept surveillance on both the girls. He had let Terry keep the knife; it seemed to discourage Billie Jean from thoughts of assault.

He didn't know what he wanted to do. Vague plans, half-formed, flitted through his mind. Maybe slip into some half-sized town in the Pacific Northwest, pick a common sort of name, slowly accumulate documentation for it and keep out of trouble so they wouldn't have cause to fingerprint him.

Sudden agony bolted him out of the car. Terry came off the porch and walked toward him. He watched her: every move she made was vital and alive. Laced with hurts, he arched his back.

"What's wrong?"

"I've got a goddamn charley horse."

"I'm sorry—can I do anything?"

He straightened slowly and stared at her. "Look, I'm the

kidnaper, you're the kidnapee   remember?"

She said, "I don't think I'm afraid of you any more. If I ever was. What are you going to do?"

"I don't know," he admitted.

"You'll take the car and run, of course. Leave me here. But I don't want to be left here with her." She gave Billie Jean, across the street pouting, a slantwise look.

"Okay, maybe I'll take her with me a ways, put her off the bus someplace else."

"That wouldn't be too smart, would it?"

"Why not?"

"She'll be found if you leave her alone on some desert road. She'll be arrested and she hasn't got the brains to keep quiet. She'll tell them everything."

"I guess so. What choice have I got? Kill her?"

"Could you?"

"No," he said, not even hesitating. He made a face and got back down under the steering wheel and poked his knife up among the wires. Sooner or later he would have to hit the right combination; there were only so many wires leading into the ignition switch. He had cut them all, stripped the insulation with the pocket knife and twisted wires together until they began to break with metal fatigue. Sweat was sticky in the small of his back, in his palms, in his crotch, on his lips and throat. He talked in exasperated bursts while he worked. "I keep feeling Floyd like a weight on me. A goddamn ghost or something. I knew he wouldn't come back—as soon as Georgie died I knew it but I didn't have the guts to do anything. The bastard can't live unless he makes everything dead around him."

He lowered his arms to rest and lifted his head. She was still there when he twisted his face to locate her. It was no good: his muscles were cramping again, he had to stand up. He sat up on the doorsill and tugged up his baggy socks and got to his feet. "I don't feel too great about leaving you here, either."

A piece of a smile shaped her mouth. "I'm sorry. You sort of got stuck with me, didn't you? Like a blind date."

Mitch was sweat-drenched; he felt greenish and sick. "Floyd figured it out real good. I can't even turn myself in to the cops.

The cops believe facts—and the facts about this are as phony as a three-dollar bill. Two people dead and a kidnaping and a missing half million dollars. They'd throw me in hock and throw away the key."

"You talk like somebody jumping out a window. It's not the end of the world, Mitch. Don't throw in the towel."

"All suggestions," he said acidly, "gratefully welcomed." He got in the car on his back and reached for the wires again. His fingers trembled wildly. The merciless orange sun beat down vengefully.

Terry's smoky voice came down to him, low but hard. "Let's not just mope around and bleed about it, Mitch. What's important is to keep a grip on yourself. Look—the thing to do is go after Floyd and get the money away from him. He doesn't deserve it."

He sat up, banging his head on the steering column; he emerged and stared. "What are you talking about?"

"Go after him, Mitch. You know where he went, don't you?"

"Floyd? He's a barracuda—he'd swallow me whole."

"I'll go with you. I'll help."

"You'll what?"

"I'll go with you. Let me go with you."

He gaped at her.

Her face hardened; she lowered her eyes. "I want my father to go on thinking I'm dead, for a little while at least."

He blinked at her, dumbfounded; she said earnestly; "I can't explain it all in a sentence, Mitch. But I want to teach him a lesson he'll never forget. I want to punish him for—for a lot of things, I suppose. If you were a psychiatrist you could find all kinds of names for it. Maybe it's bitchy and mean and neurotic and sick. But I want him to think I'm dead. I want him to *cry!*"

She turned away from him until he couldn't see her face. He took a step forward but her back registered his advance; he stopped and opened his mouth, and closed it.

Terry said in a small voice, "If we run fast the world can't catch us, Mitch. We can get the money from Floyd and disappear somewhere, together."

He swallowed. For want of anything more coherent to say he mumbled, "I wouldn't take that money on a Christmas tree if it's got Floyd attached to it. He'd grind us up into hamburgers."

"No he won't. You can figure something out."

"I'm not that long on brains. Floyd can think circles around me."

"No." She turned to face him. "You're good, Mitch. Better than you think you are."

"Am I?"

"You know you are. You just needed to have someone tell you."

He wondered if he would ever emerge from this nightmare. Her voice pounded at him: "Go after him, Mitch. What else can you do? There's nothing else. Go after him—and I'll come with you."

He shook his head slowly, not ready to catch up with the speed of her resolution. "Hell—what about her?"

"We'll take her with us, at least as far as the border. He did go to Mexico, didn't he?"

"Yah." He turned and brooded at Billie Jean's squat shape across the road. "Do you really think we can do it?"

"I think we have to try."

Fastening his mind onto it, he got back down into the car and pushed wires together—and the starter popped and spun. Startled, he jerked back. He touched the wires again and the starter whirred. He grinned insanely and bent his head against the accelerator pedal and touched the wires again. The engine started with a rattle and began to hum. Disregarding the low-amperage current that tingled in his fingers, he pulled the starter wire away, marking in his mind that it was the red one, and sat up. He banged his head again.

"Did you hurt yourself?"

"I always do." He held one hand to his head, climbed to his feet and said, "What the hell. We might as well."

She looked almost amused; she knew she had shamed him into it. If *she* was game for it, how could he refuse? *Easy*, he thought *—I could use my head.* But when he looked at her he suddenly knew he couldn't.

He called Billie Jean. Hands impudently on hips, she took her insolent time, walking slowly forward with writhing buttocks. Her dress, wrinkled and creased and filthy, was stretched tight across her fullnesses; she came up and flicked her body at him.

"You get in back."

"Huh? That seat's built for little kids and dogs. Midgets."

"Sit sideways," he said. "Or would you rather I left you here to starve?"

Billie Jean's eyes shifted toward Terry and back. "You cooked up something with her?"

He opened the little door. "Get in."

"There's something you two know that I don't know."

"Yeah," he said. "We're going after the money. You want some of it, don't you?"

"You mean going after Floyd?" she said, incredulous.

"Why not?" He tried to sound casual. "Half a million bucks, Billie Jean. Some of it's ours."

"What about *her?*"

"She's going with us. She can't talk to anybody if she's with us."

"Why not leave her here?" Billie Jean said with quiet cunning. "Nobody for her to talk to here." Her eyelids fluttered and she rolled her body humidly toward him with an invitation that had all the subtlety of an elephant's mating trumpet.

He said, "I won't argue with you. Get in or stay here, it's all the same to me. More money for me if you don't come along to split with." With cavalier indifference he nodded gravely to Terry, watched her get into the right-hand bucket seat and went around the car to climb into the driver's seat. He slammed the door, gunned the engine and shifted into gear.

With a disgusted grunt Billie Jean climbed over the back and plumped herself down sideways with her knees up near her chin. She was still squirming to get comfortable when Mitch winked at Terry and shot the clutch. The little car bolted forward; Billie Jean shouted, "Hey!"

He left town fast on the dirt road, trailing a swirling funnel of pale dust. He kept his right hand on the knob of the floor stick-shift and became aware that Terry's hand was timidly creeping toward his. He had not been able to figure her out; his feelings about her were contradictory but he was no longer able to ignore the way she was constantly in his mind, raging like a fever. He glanced at her and saw that she was watching him, her hair blowing wildly in the wind.

He felt better on the move. The wind roared around the speeding open car; he had its power in his hands, he felt more in control of things. It was the first time in days when he had enjoyed any sense of self-confidence at all. Fleetingly he even entertained the heady thought that perhaps he could best Floyd Rymer after all. He would have to figure out the way to do it.

They reached the paved county road and turned west toward the Nogales highway. So far they hadn't seen another car. The posted speed limit was sixty; at seventy the state police would give chase—if they detected the speeding car, and if they were in a mood for it; Mitch, with his attention whipping frequently to the rear-view mirror, was doing eighty-five. At that speed the little car bounced hard on its spartan springs; the wind flailed his face and he had to concentrate on keeping the car on the road, alert for chuck-holes and loose drifts of sand. Terry's warm palm rested on the back of his hand; she sat at ease, not worried by his driving, and her confidence in him gave him lift. In the mirror he could see Billie Jean press her palms to her temples to keep her hair from lashing her face; her eyes were shut against the wind and she was smiling with her mouth open in sensual enjoyment. He wondered what was going on inside her head; he knew very little about Billie Jean, really—partly because he knew very little about the facts of her background, but mainly because it was impossible to make assumptions about her. She was, perhaps, as simple as she seemed—but her simplicity was shaped by a different pattern from the ones he was accustomed to. He had never known anyone as freely immoral, as innocent of conscience: she was capable of extreme brutality but somehow it was utterly without malice. In that respect she was eerily like Floyd. Neither of them would have any compunctions at all about killing a fly—or a man—but at the same time neither of them would trouble to commit the necessary violence unless the fly, or the man, happened to be annoying them; and even when they did commit violence they would do it with an almost apathetic insouciance, uncolored by even the faintest shading of animus or relish or anxiety. Back there this morning Billie Jean had been perfectly willing to kill Terry—had tried to, on the porch—but only because she had felt there was a practical reason for it: she had, or at least she displayed, no personal feelings whatever toward Terry as a human being.

When they approached the main-traveled road he eased the speed to sixty-five. Cars began to appear—station wagons and dusty Cadillacs and rattletrap pickup trucks. He averted his face as they passed. He took the left turn into the wide highway, enjoyed the way the little car cornered, and was taken by surprise—because he wasn't used to small-car driving—when an onrushing Greyhound bus went by in the opposite direction and rocked the sports car in its wake of hissing wind.

Approaching Nogales he obeyed the speed-limit signs, which brought him down to fifty, then thirty-five; driving the high hillside bend with rocks above on the right and the Santa Cruz river below on his left, he said to Terry, "Have you got any money in your bag?"

"I did. Unless somebody went through it while we were back there."

He was hoping nobody had. She pawed through her handbag, took out a red leather purse-wallet and snapped it open. "It's still here. What do you know."

"How much?"

"More than you might think," she said with a small grin. "My daddy got me in the habit of carrying a lot of cash. Just in case of emergency, he always says—or in case you see something you want to buy and they don't take credit cards."

He swung right into a side street that angled between gas stations and warehouses. "How much?"

She was counting, frowning, moving her lips. He glimpsed the edges of twenty-dollar bills. She gave a nervous little laugh and said, "I almost hate to admit it. Almost three hundred dollars."

"Don't apologize," he said grimly.

He bought a $235 Ford from a used-car lot and drove it back

to the quiet street where they had parked the little red car. He took everything out of the trunk and packed it away in the Ford. Terry helped him put up the canvas top of the sports car; they couldn't lock it because they didn't have a key. There were no No-Parking signs in sight; he judged it would be quite some time before the parked car would draw attention. He shooed Billie Jean and Terry into the Ford and they drove down through town, had to wait ten minutes in the queue of cars at the bottleneck, and went on through the international border with a nod and a smile at the Mexican guards who waved them through, as they waved all cars through. Mitch said, "That part was easy. The rough stuff comes down below. They'll let anybody into the border towns. It's when you get out of town on the highway that you've got to show your tourist permit. Which we haven't got."

Terry said, "I've got my passport with me. They'll accept that."

"Not for all three of us."

Thinking on it, he drove on slowly through thick horsefly-crowds of pedestrians—tourists and peddlers. They went past Canal Street, which climbed steeply to the right, a row of whorehouses with girls sitting on the shaded porches. He said uncomfortably, "This is as far as I've ever been. Where do we go from here, to get out of town?"

"Down past the bull ring—keep going." Terry gave him a wry look.

The Ford was an oil-burner. Its radio didn't work. It needed springs and shock-absorbers and he hesitated to think what else. But at least it ran—and it was clean, for the moment. It would take the cops a long time to trace them through the car. Not that they couldn't do it, eventually. But eventually, he thought. *Eventually. . . . Who the hell knows?* He looked at Terry, on the far side of the seat trying to comb the tangles out of her hair. He said, "Where's the entry station where they check your papers?"

"Four or five miles down the road after we get out of town."

"What's the countryside like?"

She had to think about it; finally she said, "Kind of flat and deserty. It's the other side of these hills."

"In other words they could see somebody on foot for quite a distance?"

"I'm afraid they could," she answered, indicating by her reply that she understood what he had in mind. "You'd have a long walk."

"How long? Five miles? Ten?"

"I don't know, Mitch. It's awfully flat to the south of it. Of course it would all depend whether they happened to be looking out in that direction."

"We can't take the chance they won't." He chewed his lip. The road curled past the high bull ring—a coliseum papered with colorful posters—and ran on south through a widening canyon alongside the railroad tracks. The dark blue car absorbed sun heat through the roof; he drove with all the windows open, his left arm propped up. The traffic was steady and light, mostly old American cars and Volkswagens. The Ford fitted in beautifully.

The last adobe buildings receded behind them and were absorbed in the mirror's rear-view by the dun-colored hills. The road ran up a long easy grade ahead and disappeared over it. Terry said, "It's down on the flats beyond this hill."

He pulled over to the shoulder before they reached the crest; got out and walked up just far enough to be able to see past the crest. From this high vantage-point he could sweep a panorama that sprawled a good many miles toward various mountain ranges, haze-blue in the distance. The road ran down the slope ahead of him two or three miles to a permanent roadblock and a solitary cubical building flying the Mexican flag; beyond, the highway ribboned south for miles before it twisted out of sight.

He pinched his mouth irritably and walked back to the car. "That's no good. We'll have to wait for nightfall. Then you drive through the checkpoint while Billie Jean and I walk around the back of the place. We'll make a wide circle, a mile or so—you'll have to wait for us on the other side."

Billie Jean said, "You mean we got to kill the whole day here? It's too damned hot."

"We'll go back to Nogales and get some lunch and some beer."

"Yeah," Billie Jean said. "I could use some."

He made a tight U-turn and drove back the way they had come. Terry's hand rested on his thigh as he drove.

CHAPTER **Fourteen**

Somehow Earle Conniston's office—which had rarely been occupied by more than two people at a time during Conniston's reign—had become the center of the household. They had all four congregated there on the night of Earle's death; it seemed natural that they keep coming back to it.

Halfway through this insomniac night they were gathered in the office—four people in the same room but not together. Carl Oakley was striding back and forth. Louise Conniston sat pushing her ice cubes around with a swizzle stick. Frankie Adams, graven-faced, was twisting his knuckles and chewing on a pencil and frowning at a newspaper crossword puzzle in his lap. Diego Orozco sat in his favorite straight chair with hands on knees, the weight of his huge belly sagging against his thighs.

Louise wore a rustling silk dress. When she twisted in the chair to look at Oakley her breasts handled the cloth seductively. "Why don't you sit down?"

"I think better on my feet."

"You're nervous. You're making me nervous, so you must be nervous." Her words ran together carelessly; she was tight, or high—Oakley had never pinned down the distinction.

Frankie Adams said, "What's the capital of Ecuador? La Paz? Five letters."

"That's in Bolivia," Oakley said absently.

Orozco muttered, "Quito."

"Yeah. Thanks."

Oakley tugged back his sleeve and looked at his watch. Two seconds later if someone had asked him the time he wouldn't have been able to answer. He resumed pacing with his hands in his pockets.

Adams uttered a monosyllabic curse and slapped the pencil down on the newspaper. "I can't do these damn things."

Louise said, "It beats hell out of me how you two legal and detective geniuses can identify both those dead bodies and still come up with nothing."

"We've got their names," Oakley said, "and for the moment that's all we've got. It's worth about as much as a nun's virginity —we've got it but what good is it?"

Orozco said in his unperturbed growl, "We'll have more information coming in pretty quick. My stringers are working up files on them."

"Sure—sure," Louise said. "But what happens then?"

"I'm not clairvoyant," Oakley said. "All I can tell you is they didn't leave her there dead. Which means she may be alive."

Louise knocked back her drink. "But if they let her go why haven't we heard from her? And if they didn't, why didn't they?"

Oakley didn't answer. He went to the big leather chair and sat back, crossed his legs at right angles, laced his hands behind his head and knitted his brows. He kept looking at the telephone. All evening he had swung pendulantly from one extreme of emotion to the other—elation, despondency. They had found the spliced phone wires early in the afternoon and after that things had moved fast: they had found the two naked bodies in the ghost town before sundown. A discreet contact of Orozco's in the Tucson police lab had run the fingerprints through for identification and Oakley had still been on his after-dinner coffee when the replies had come through—Orozco's team had worked with remarkable dispatch. But what did it add up to? Oakley had even looked them both up in every one of the phone books in Earle's cabinets. No Theodore Luke, no George Rymer. The two names hung suspended in a vacuum.

None of the radio direction-finders had picked up any signals from the bugged suitcase. The two sets of tire tracks in the ghost-town barn meant very little, if anything—one set belonged to Terry's Daimler, which had not been sighted anywhere, and the other set consisted of worn mismatched tires of a brand not used on new cars. Thus there was no way to identify the make of the larger car. Orozco's operatives had put out the word on the red sports job but that, Oakley thought bitterly, was like looking for a needle in Nebraska. Arizona was crawling with two-seater cars and half of them were red.

Theodore Luke had a vague record of three arrests and one suspended sentence, on charges of simple assault and drunk-and-disorderly. George Rymer had a record of narcotics arrests. Both men had been musicians—New York City had refused Theodore Luke a cabaret license because of his criminal record. But there was nothing in the sum of that information to suggest that either of them had ever been involved in robberies, extortions, or any of the other varieties of crime that a lawyer might expect to find in a kidnaper's background.

It was all elusive, inconclusive, mocking. Oakley's eyes were lacquered with weary frustration.

Frankie Adams said crossly, "I'm going to bed," and left the room. Louise stirred the melting ice in her glass; Oakley watched her moodily. She caught his eye on her and she smiled, her eyes half-closed; she looked warm and lazy. She sat up and lifted her arms to fiddle with her hair. Under the silk dress her breasts stood out like torpedoes, drawing Oakley's masculine attention, arousing him and irritating him with the distraction. Louise, meeting his glance, became very still, her arms upraised; her eyes mirrored a sensual speculation. Still smiling, she yawned luxuriously and walked out of the room trailing musk.

Oakley's palms felt moist. He felt his face color when he caught Orozco looking at him, bland-faced. *He sees everything,* Oakley thought, and made a note to quit taking Orozco for granted—lunatic *chicano* land-schemes aside, Orozco was a vigilant and clever man, possibly dangerous. *The inscrutable Mexican,* he thought dryly: Orozco had superb control, he never let you see anything he didn't want you to see.

They kept vigil by the telephone, the prime umbilical. It did not ring. Oakley began to feel drowsy; he hadn't had much sleep in the past three days. *Getting old*, he thought, and felt solemn and sad, regretting all the things he had not done when he was young and all the things he would never do, either because of lack of time or because of lack of passion. He had never been a man of passions; he saw himself as a repressed man, cool, channeled, deliberate. He thought of the unsubtle suggestion Louise had left hanging in the air *(anything but inscrutable)* and it focused his weary thinking once again on the fact that he was no longer young, that it was time to settle for something less than the unachievable perfection of a Technicolor marriage with violins. Something made not in heaven but in kitchen, bed, living room. It seemed a wry irony that his reputation was that of a blade. He couldn't even remember most of their names—an endless procession of soft humid bodies with interchangeable faces. It was always easiest that way: no attachments, no commitments, no passions. Yet it gave him little joy, left him ragged, sapped his energies—the timeless ritual of pretense and mutual seduction. Once he had met a girl in a bar who had said to him refreshingly, "You don't have to buy me drinks and dinner. I only want to get laid." Blunt, forthright—yet she had been attractive, young, charming. But she had been just passing through. They were all just passing through.

He came back to Louise. Young, attractive, widowed, sensual. Rich besides. If he played his cards right she would marry him; he was certain of it. But it wouldn't do. He could endure a marriage without love; he probably wasn't capable of making any other kind. But marriage to Louise would be a duel—a constant abrasive antagonism; a clashing of desires, the headstrong against the reasoned, the passionate against the temperate. He didn't need a Louise. He needed a milkmaid.

His reveries began to distend and wander; he leaned back in the tilting chair and put his feet up on Earle's desk, glanced drowsily at Orozco and closed his eyes. . . . The morning sun beamed across the desk and he came awake with a start, searched guiltily for Orozco and learned the room was empty. He mouthed a mild oath, lowered his feet to the floor, sat up.

His tongue felt dry and bloated; he scraped a hand over his stubbled chin and blinked ferociously, cupped a big hand around the back of his neck and reared his head back until the bones creaked.

He crossed the hall, tired and rumpled, and found Orozco sitting on his bed with a fat paw across the telephone receiver and a slight frown on his face. Orozco's chin lifted: "I came in here to take the calls. Didn't want to wake you."

"Thanks, Diego." It had been an unexpected kindness. Orozco kept displaying new facets, each of which further eroded the slothful impassive image.

Orozco said, "Things are starting to break."

"Good. Can it wait ten minutes? I've got to wash the sleep off."

"Go ahead."

He stripped to his underwear and closed himself into the bathroom to shower and shave and clean his teeth. He felt stiff and sore, with a particularly insistent ache in the muscles of his neck and knees; *Getting old,* he thought, and realized the phrase was becoming an obsessive repetition in his lexicon. It didn't help to look in the mirror; the haggard face was not reassuring. He tried to remember how long it had been since he had really looked at his face in a mirror. When he shaved or combed his hair he never looked at himself to the extent of appraising the whole. Now he saw the creases that bracketed his mouth, the beginnings of sag under the eyes, the crow's feet, the spreading gray in the hair. It was still a photogenic visage, younger than his years, but the flesh beneath his chin was beginning to loosen and he thought with a harsh defensiveness which he immediately knew was designed to mask deep-rooted panic, *I'm forty-six, after all.*

He hurried out of the mirrored room, climbed into clean-pressed clothes and said, "I could use a cup of coffee."

"So could I." Orozco went to the kitchen with him and stood hip-shot against the counter while Oakley searched the unfamiliar cabinets for a coffeepot and finally settled for a covered cooking pan in which he set out water to boil. He glanced at the electric clock above the door—seven fifteen—and took down a jar of instant coffee and a pair of cups. "You take anything in it?"

"Just black."

"Me too." *Black for my youth: I'm in mourning.* He made a wry face at his own melodramatic sourness and turned, leaning against the refrigerator with his arms folded across his chest. "Well?"

"They found Terry's car in Nogales. Parked on a side street. Nothing much left in it but there were fingerprints all over it and we're running them through for identification. One funny thing, though—somebody'd hot-wired it. So the prints we come up with may belong to some clown who stole it from the kidnapers."

"Swell."

"There'll be a plane coming in sometime in the next half-hour with dossiers on the two dead guys and the people they associated with. One of them had a brother—they all three worked in the same nightclub combo. There was a fourth guy in it too. That may be our gang."

"A band of musicians?"

"They lost their last job in Tucson a few weeks ago. The skinny one we found dead was an addict. I don't know what else he was but a habit his size would take a hell of a lot of money. It was his brother that was the bandleader. It adds up for motive and opportunity, Carl. They needed money bad, they had no work."

"And they're as slippery as watermelon seeds. We've got to do better than this, Diego."

"It's coming along," Orozco said mildly. "We'll crack it. You remember that voice on the phone—too much conceit there. When you get an amateur who thinks he knows more about strategy than Clausewitz you got a character who's going to make mistakes. When he does we'll have him."

Oakley took the lid off the boiling water and poured. "Maybe. But I can't stand sitting around here waiting. Get a man in here to keep an eye on Adams and Louise. I'm going back to that ghost town with you. Maybe we'll find something they missed yesterday."

An hour later he was ready to go when the phone rang. He answered it and heard the words he had been waiting for: "Carl? You've got your uptick. The market opened with Conniston up."

"Good. You've got your instructions."

He had to make a dozen phone calls to put the machinery in motion; now that things had begun to stir he found that he had snapped out of his melancholy dirge. It was like the opening rounds of a courtroom battle. After the morose night of stage fright he was at last in the arena of action; it brought him up on his toes, settled his mind into a new clarity of focus, rekindled his confidence and decisiveness. Before, trying to keep control of the whole mess had been like trying to hold onto his hat in a gusty wind. The risks had appeared formidable, the juggling task a formidable one. But now he moved with sure firm steps. He phoned Earle's doctor, and while they waited for the physician he held a curt briefing session in Earle's office, instructing Louise and Frankie Adams—in Orozco's absence—in what they were to tell the doctor. The doctor arrived at ten, acquisitive and tame; the mendacious ritual was attended to and Oakley walked the doctor out to his car: "You'll receive the—fee—in cash, of course, and I'd prefer it if you didn't deposit it in any bank accounts. Put it in a lock box and spend it where nobody knows you. It isn't reported from our end and we won't want you reporting it as coming from us. You never know when they'll hit you with a spot-check out of the computer."

"Of course." The doctor was urbane, avuncular. "I'll arrange everything with the funeral director. The embalming will be done here if that's satisfactory. I presume you'll want him buried here on the ranch?"

"I believe he wanted cremation. It's in his will."

"Excellent," the doctor said, and added with a frank smile, "We wouldn't want there to be any possibility of exhumation for autopsy, would we?"

When the doctor had left, Oakley called his office and told his secretary of Conniston's death. There was a brief exchange of appropriate solicitudes and eulogized phrases after which Oakley gave instructions for the release to the press of the news of

Conniston's death. Then he left instructions with the ranch staff to admit no journalists through the gates or into the main house; he would, he said, issue a formal statement on behalf of the family tomorrow afternoon—in the meantime Conniston's wife and daughter, he said, were too grieved to meet with the press. Three of Orozco's men stood guard around the house to insure that no one disturbed the weeping widow and orphan.

By afternoon, he knew, the death of the tycoon would be known on Wall Street. The price of Conniston stock would dive through the floor. Oakley's dummy-fronts would cover his short sales and use the money from that to buy up the stock again at its crippled price. He estimated it would take him about thirty-six hours to gain control. The key to his scheme was the fact that Earle had not owned a controlling interest in his own business —he had been expanding so fast he had to sell stock to raise capital; and he had made every effort to see that large blocks of stock never accumulated in the hands of possible rivals, even members of his own board of directors. Conniston had held about twenty-three percent of the outstanding common stock in Conniston Industries, the holding conglomerate which owned all the Conniston subsidiaries. That stock would go to Louise and to Terry if she were still alive. Thousands of stockholders owned the remaining seventy-seven percent—mutual funds, private investors, insurance portfolios. Oakley already owned eight percent; he needed forty-three percent of the rest—less than two thirds of the stock which would become available in the impending mini-panic. When the news of Conniston's death hit the ticker the big funds would be the first to sell, trying to liquidate before the inevitable plunge. Their quick sales of large blocks would further depress the price. Even if the Exchange suspended trading in the stock Oakley's brokers would pick it up over the counter. The beauty of it was that Oakley was not an officer of Conniston Industries—he had been Conniston's personal attorney but held no official title—and he owned less than ten percent of the stock; thus, in legal terms, he was not an "insider" and was not required to divulge his activities to the SEC. He had broken no law except to conceal the facts in Conniston's death; and it was hardly likely anyone would reveal his part in that. All of them had too much to lose.

Luck, he thought, swinging back toward the ecstatic extreme. It was all working out perfectly. . . . But later, driving back from Soledad with the Rymer file on the Cadillac seat between them, he felt a sudden chill when Orozco said, "My boys could work a lot faster if I told them what we're really up against. They don't even know it's a kidnap caper."

"Are you suggesting we tell them?"

"No. I imagine by now it's too late for you ever to reveal the kidnaping to anybody. You'd have to admit how you took advantage of it to get control of Conniston's business."

Oakley stiffened. He held his tongue for a long while, thinking fast. The highway two-laned down through the cow-country valley and in spite of the air-conditioning he felt the sudden pressure of the day's torpid heat. Dark sweat-circles stained the armpits of his shirt. Unnerved, he said, "Maybe you're jumping to conclusions, Diego."

"I'm a detective, remember? Maybe I heard some of those phone calls you made this morning."

"You mean you listened in?"

"I'd rather call it monitoring the conversation." Orozco turned in the seat and tapped Oakley on the shoulder. "Maybe what really worries you is the possibility Terry's still alive."

"What's *that* supposed to mean?"

"If she's alive, *she* knows about the kidnaping. How you going to shut her up?"

Oakley showed his teeth around his unlit cigar. "I'm not that cold-blooded. What do you take me for?"

"I honestly don' know, Carl. I ain't got you figured out yet."

"Let me know when you do," he said, recklessly vicious.

"I'll do that."

The road took them east between yellow-grass rolls of cattle country. Some distance ahead and a bit to the right they could see the gray rise of the Chiricahuas beyond the cliff of Biscuit Mountain. All forest up there, and abandoned old diggings; you could ride forty miles horseback through those mountains and never cross a road, never raise the lights of a human habitation. Oakley, who had room in his soul for a streak of ardent conservationism, knew those mountains from boyhood and felt, once in a while, a keen sadness at the passing of such beasts as the timber wolf and the mountain lion, which had been hunted relentlessly out of the region.

Is it a sign of encroaching old age that the mind starts to wander? He squirmed his buttocks back in the seat, sitting up straighter, scowling.

Orozco said, "How come a character with all Conniston's money didn't have a big staff of house servants and all? Mrs. Conniston *like* to cook? All's I've seen around there is the housekeeper coming in during the day."

"Earle had a few spartan streaks. He liked to fool with electric wiring and plumbing himself—he did all the repairs around the house, he was a pretty fair Sunday carpenter and painter. They used to have two or three live-in servants but Earle"—he paused, and concluded lamely—"got tired of them." No point in revealing to Orozco that a few months ago Earle had decided he didn't trust any of them. Another sign of paranoia he had missed at the time. Storm signals had gone up all over the place, he realized now, but it had taken him the longest time to start recognizing them. Once you formed in your mind a picture of a person it was hard to dislodge it; you were reluctant to change your feelings about him.

He glanced sidewise at Orozco and felt a little better for knowing that Orozco's mind could drift off the subject at hand too.

But not for long. Orozco said, "Sonoita coming up soon. Stop a minute and I'll check in with my boys."

The pavement unrolled into Sonoita two miles ahead—a crossroads which could only be called a town by an act of charity. There were half a dozen buildings around the road-crossing, a few houses scattered on the slopes farther away, and a great litter of weathered high-fenced corrals and loading pens by the railroad tracks. From the four-cornered intersection roads ran north toward Tucson, west toward Nogales, south toward the Elgin cow-country, and east across the Army's missile-artillery range to Fort Huachuca and old Tombstone, the onetime bailiwick of fabulous ones like John Slaughter and

Wyatt Earp. It was a country full of violent history. At a local rodeo in Sonoita only a few years ago two ranchers, disputing their claims to the same Nogales girl, had shot it out in a gunfight the traditions of which went back to feudal duels. The antagonists had been an Anglo and a *chicano;* the Anglo, a wealthy rancher, had armed himself with a Mannlicher rifle, while the *chicano,* an only slightly less wealthy Mexican-American rancher, had brought a twelve-gauge double-barrel shotgun. The Anglo had taken advantage of his firepower by opening fire before they had walked within shotgun range of one another. Nonetheless the jury—all gringos—had denied the state's murder charge, found that defendant had acted in self-defense, and freed him. There had been a round of ranch-parties in celebration afterward, to which no Mexicans came; the valley, cut by the Santa Cruz River, was known accurately enough as the Santa Booze Valley; the *chicanos* had burned down a few barns in angry rage but the partying gringos had been too cheerful about the whole thing to retaliate. And this was the country in which Orozco wanted the gringos to give the land back to the *chicanos.* Oakley gave him a wry glance when he pulled over by the green-painted roadside phone booth.

He waited in the car while the fat man made his calls. He thumbed through the dossier on the Rymer group again but it didn't hold his attention. He checked the time—just coming up on two o'clock—and twisted the radio knob to catch the news-on-the-hour. A plane crash in Indiana, an airliner highjacking in Greece, Russian rumblings over the Czechoslovak hippies, a Chinese H-bomb test in Sinkiang Province, terrorist bombings of government radio stations in Bolivia; and now on the state and local scene, Democratic gubernatorial candidate flays flabby record of incumbent Governor, newspaper strike continues, three-alarm fire in downtown Tucson slum dwelling. The newscast gave twenty seconds near the end to Earle Conniston; the tycoon had, the announcer said in his relentlessly smiling voice, "succumbed to a sudden illness during the night."

Oakley switched it off, satisfied. Orozco came waddling back toward the car, got in and closed the door with a grunt. "Stay put a minute—I got to make one more call."

†† 149

"Qué pasó?"

"We're gettin' there—we're gettin' there. The Baird kid bought a ten-year-old Ford from a used-car lot in Nogales yesterday afternoon, not too far from where we found Terry's car. The bleeper we planted in that suitcase showed up headed west on Highway Two across Sonora, toward Altar and Rocky Point. And here's the funny thing. Terry Conniston went through the Mexican checkpoint five miles south of Nogales last night. Driving a ten-year-old Ford. Alone."

"Alone?"

"By herself."

Oakley closed his eyes momentarily. "I don't get that."

"Well, look here, maybe they planted the fear of God in her. They could have walked around the station while she went through it. Picked her up on the far side."

"How in hell could they persuade her to keep her mouth shut?"

"I got no idea. Thing is, she did it. She can get anyplace in Mexico on that road, just about. It's the main highway down through Hermosillo and Guaymas. Or she could turn right on Highway Two—the same road the suitcase took."

Oakley tried to picture the map in his mind. "Where would that get them?"

"Eventually to Rocky Point. On the Golf of California. They could maybe hire a fishing boat there and head for just about anyplace. I sent a couple operatives down there in a seaplane. Meanwhile we've got two boys in a car at this end of Highway Two. That should bottle them up between the two ends of the road, unless they got through Rocky Point already and put out to sea—but there's no sign they did. The bleeper ain't showed up at Rocky Point. I'd hazard a wild guess they all rendezvoused together at some town along the road, Altar or Caborca, stopped overnight. They could still show up any time this afternoon at Rocky Point. Now I got to get back on the wire and give orders. You're payin' the bills, you're the boss. How you want us to handle it?"

Oakley was still absorbing it. *She's alive.* His contradictory feelings made him react sluggishly but finally he said, "We'll handle it ourselves. The less your men know, the better. We'll drive down there and follow their route—if we catch up we'll deal with them and if they go on to Rocky Point then your men can keep tabs on them until you and I get there. I don't want outsiders or police involved."

"It's your party," Orozco said, and unlatched the door.

Oakley said, "Tell your people in Nogales to have things ready for us in an hour. We'll need guns and a radio direction-finder to zero in on the suitcase."

"Okay," Orozco said. If he was displeased he didn't give much indication, but he didn't look overjoyed. He got out of the car and tramped to the phone booth. Oakley settled back in the seat. Whatever the outcome now, there was at least a measure of relief in the prospect of action.

CHAPTER Fifteen

In the heat Billie Jean sat with her legs wide apart, fanning herself with a folded roadmap. Mitch formed a loose fist, shifting his glance from her to Terry, who stood near the gasoline pumps under the concrete station awning.

Sleeplessness laid a semitransparent glaze over Mitch's eyes; he had to keep blinking. Wracked by bruises and sore muscles, he contained his irritability badly. They had been stuck in this woebegone gas station seven hours.

The grease monkey came up out of the pit under the car wiping his hands on a filthy rag. He was a diminutive old man with the high-cheeked face of a pureblood Indian, the jet-black hair and old-copper skin. A broad grin showed the gaps in his teeth. "Oll ehfeexed," he said happily. "Jew gonna pagar een dolors o een pesos?"

"Dollars." Mitch's hand plunged into his trouser side-pocket and crumpled a bill. "How much?"

"Eh?"

"Cuanto?"

"Oh. *Sí. Cómo, cómo—*" The mechanic counted on his grease-black fingers, his lips moving. *"Cuarenta . . . dos . . . catorce . . . por ocho."* He frowned and shook his head, and suddenly threw his head back, beaming. *"Doce dolares, por favor.* Ees twelve dollars." He added with an apologetic shrug, "Would be maybe not so mahch, bot hod to ehfeex the *calceta* and the *pompa* too, jew know? The, ah, the—*chingadera*, I donno the name een Eenglish, jew know?"

"I don't want to hear about it," Mitch muttered, and fumbled twelve dollars into the blackened palm. He wheeled past the girls and said crankily, "Come on—come on."

He rolled the car on west through the rocky desert hills, wondering how long the old grease-monkey's patchwork job would hold the water pump together before it burst again. He kept it down to forty-five most of the time, except on the downhill slopes, hoping the water temperature wouldn't rise high enough to blow another hole by steam pressure. In the back seat Billie Jean said crankily, "Jesus H. Christ. I never been so sticky damn hot in my life."

"Shut up."

Terry touched his arm but he gave her a stony look and she withdrew her hand. They limped west in silence after that.

According to the map they had picked up at the gas station, Caborca was a smallish town (*población* 5,000-7,500) on the Rio Asunción. There was, however, no sign of a river anywhere in sight when they reached the sign which said HEROICA CABORCA. The appelation, Terry explained, commemorated the occasion in the 1850s when a hundred Yankee filibusters had invaded Sonora, planning to capture it and annex it to the United States; they had been besieged here by the local populace, abetted by several companies of militia, and finally forced to surrender, whereupon the Mexicans had lined them up against the wall and slaughtered them with rifle fire, after which the corpses were stripped of gold teeth and rings and left naked to the village pigs and goats. According to legend it had taken more than a year for the stench to dissipate. It had been the high point, if not the only memorable moment, in the town's four-hundred-year history. The severed head of the filibuster leader had been pickled and placed on display in a jar. It was probably around somewhere, still. The walls of the old Franciscan church were still pocked with bullet holes.

The town clustered against the shoulders of several steep round hills, surrounded by scratch-poor country, all weathered clay and dry brittle clumps of brush. Here and there were painfully irrigated vegetable patches. Flocks of gaunt sheep drifted listlessly across the open desert. Dogs lay in the shade watching through bloodshot eyes when Mitch reached the outskirts of town and slowed to a crawl to make way, horn blasting, through a thickness of chickens clucking in the road.

Ahead on the right stood an apparition: a brand-new motel, complete with plastic, chrome, neon, and swimming pool. Mitch stopped in front of it and eyed the cars parked in the lot. None was Floyd's Oldsmobile. Anyhow, he thought, Floyd wouldn't be likely to stop at a conspicuous place like this.

He drove on into town. The streets were narrow, once paved but now holed and dusted. There were occasional cobbled sidewalks. The adobe structures, rammed together like city slum buildings, were painted ludicrous colors—pinks, yellows, greens. Poverty didn't have to be soot-gray. Slow-moving women with black hair tied back in buns and dusty dresses with flowing long skirts stared at Mitch as if he were a movie director looking for extras to cast in a Pancho Villa film. Men in cowboy hats sat somnolent in shady doorways like characters in cartoons of Old Mexico. It was the siesta hour.

There were a few cars parked with two wheels on the sidewalk—mainly pickups and station wagons, the old ones with real wooden bodies. Mitch didn't see the Olds anywhere; he hardly expected to. Floyd wouldn't make it that easy.

He pulled up next to a young man in pachuco-tight Levi's and stuck his head out the window; he spoke with care, drawing his lips back over his teeth in exaggerated enunciation:

"Por favor, amigo, dónde está la farmacia?"

The youth grinned and rattled off something, adding wild arm-and-hand signals like a ship's semaphore signalman. Mitch flushed and heard Terry laugh at him: "He says it's two blocks down and turn right and go across the plaza."

"Okay," Mitch said, *"Gracias."*

"De nada," the youth said, and stood grinning until they drove out of his sight.

Mitch said, "What's so funny about us?"

"Maybe he just likes to smile," Billie Jean said. "Man, those tight pants, you could sure see how he was hung."

Mitch didn't glance at Terry; he felt redness creep up his neck. Terry said, "You've got a way with words, Billie Jean."

"Shit—you making fun of me? Maybe I don't like your high-and-mighty, either, you ever think of that?"

The plaza enclosed a park with a dead lawn and two or three palm trees. Mitch drove around it and found a parking space in front of the pharmacy. A pulse began to thud in his throat. He got the .38 out of the glove compartment and shoved it in his pocket—it was empty but the whole world didn't have to know that. *I should've remembered to buy cartridges in Nogales. Maybe they've got some here.*

It was just like the photograph, von Roon's name painted on the sign. The door was closed and when he banged on it he got no response. He tried the knob but it was locked.

Terry said from the car window, "That's why the kid was grinning. It's siesta time—everything's closed."

Mitch backed down the three steps and came around the car and got in. "Great."

Billie Jean said, "What now, smart guy?"

"We wait for them to open up."

"Not here," Billie Jean said immediately. "Not here. Too hot in this car. Man, what's wrong with that place back there we passed with the swimming pool? I could use a jump in that pool right now."

He glanced at Terry. "That place might not be too bad an idea at that. If we can afford it."

Billie Jean said, "I got some money of my own. I'll pay my own way. Just you drive me back to that pool."

Drunk in his legs, Mitch opened the door and went in and looked around. His eyeballs seemed to scrape the sockets. The motel room was new, impersonal, sparsely filled with cheap blond furniture. It smelled stale. The drowsy desk clerk had explained with huge amusement how the motel, with its enormous carpeted lobby, had been built by gringo speculators who had assurances from the Mafia that Sonora was about to legalize gambling. The motel was to have been a gambling casino—only Sonora hadn't passed the gambling law. That had been eight or nine years ago. The gringo speculators were still scheming and the Mafia were still making promises and the motel was still losing much money. The clerk had laughed uproariously. He had cast his wizened eye at Billie Jean (Terry had remained outside in the car) and at Mitch, and he had winked and handed over the keys to two rooms. They didn't have enough money to take three rooms. Besides, it would have attracted attention.

He sat down on the bed and began to unlace his shoes. A shadow filled the door and he looked up to see Terry looking at him with an inquiring glance. He said, "You two take the other room."

"If you think I'm going to stay in a room with that female Genghis Khan you're mistaken."

"Stay here, then. God knows I'm too fagged out to be dangerous." He smiled weakly. "I feel like a two-dollar clock that somebody forgot to wind up. I don't know about you but I'm going to wash off some of this dirt before I have to start paying real estate taxes on it."

He shut himself in the bathroom, turned on the shower and let the water run until the rust cleared out of it, and scrubbed himself almost viciously. *Blood on my hands,* he thought sardonically, remembering the high-school production of *Macbeth.* "Is this a Floyd I see before me," he muttered. He washed out his drip-dry shirt and underwear in the sink and hung them, wrung out and wrinkled, across the shower bar; and went back into the main room with a bath towel wrapped around his midriff. "I feel twenty pounds lighter."

Terry sat in a rickety chair with loosely crossed legs, her hair standing out in wild disorder, looking rumpled and untidy and too tired to care. For the first time he realized she was as worn and ragged as he was; he had begun to think she was indestructible.

"Go on in and take a shower. Make you feel better."

"As soon as I get the strength," she mumbled. She glanced at him; her eyes seemed slightly glazed. "What in the hell are we doing here?"

"Sometimes I forget, myself."

"We're bananas," she said vaguely. "Stark, raving bananas."

She got up and took a moment to steady her balance, and went weaving into the bathroom.

He lay back on the bed and listened to the beat of the shower. *Ought to keep an eye on Billie Jean,* he thought distantly; and then, *To hell with her, let her look out for herself.* Everything was so muddled it didn't really matter any more. The pipedream was just that; ashes, now. Maybe Floyd was around here someplace and maybe he wasn't—what difference did it make? It would be just as easy to rob Fort Knox. In a dark fugue, a dirge, Mitch closed his eyes. He felt instantly as if he were falling down on layers of misty cushions; he heard himself whimper softly in his half-sleep and then a kind of peace settled on him.

A soft touch on his cheek brought him sharply awake. His eyes flashed open.

Terry, leaning over him, kissed him.

He got up on his elbows. She pushed him back with a slim pink arm coated with a fine gauze of soft pale hairs. She was sitting on the edge of the bed; she drew the towel tighter around her; the tip of her tongue quested her mouth corner. She looked pink and scrubbed. Inside, Mitch felt a visceral quiver, the slow coil and press of wanting her—*stupid,* he said to himself; but out of his urgency of danger, his sense of hopeless failing, came a blood need that sent spasms into him, beyond reason or sensibility.

Her eyes locked on his; her mouth became soft and lost its smile, her eyes became drowsily heavy. With a finger he brushed back a stray damp lock of her hair. He didn't want to think beyond this bed, this moment, her. He felt tranquil and sure. He pulled her down, drew her tenderly close; her head moved over his and she made a kitteny little sound in her throat and pressed against him and sucked his lower lip. Her mouth made deeper and deeper demands; he twisted, rolling her, grinding against her. She touched him—hot sensation raced through him. He pulled the towel away and laid his face in the softness of her flesh: her body, which looked like hot marble, was after all the softest of down. She pulled his head tight against her and he felt her stir, her breath coming as quick as his own; they made love with a driving hard urgency, hers matching his own.

When he lay back all the certainty drained out of him as if a plug had been pulled. A knotted muscle rippled at his jaw; he didn't look at her until she made as if to get up. Then he put out a detaining hand. He pulled her against him and spoke into the turned hollow of her neck:

"I'm sorry. You didn't deserve that—you don't deserve any part of me. I never wanted to—turn you into something cheap, something to be ashamed of."

She drew away, saying nothing. After a moment he reached for her hand. It was ice-cold. She said abruptly, "Is that how you feel? Cheap?"

"No—I didn't mean——"

"You're a puritan, Mitch. Underneath that hip exterior is a pious prude. Don't you think I wanted this as much as you did?"

He studied her gravely—the earnest wide beauty of her eyes, the soft curves of her body. Feeling almost burst his throat: he felt an overwhelming warmth course through him, an unreasoning reaching-out of his heart. "I must have been around Billie Jean too long—she's the one that makes it seem cheap. I'm sorry I said that—I didn't mean it. I don't know what I really meant. Well, look, I never said I wasn't stupid."

She lay back and smiled at the ceiling. "Don't you feel fine?"

They waited in shared nesty silence, not needing to talk, until the grinding tensions began to return, setting his nerves on edge again, dispelling the moment's grateful lassitude. Fear was a malaise never far from the surface, reminding him biliously that this wasn't an idyll but only a momentary respite.

He said, "I think you'd better get in touch with your old man. You don't have to tell him where you are but you ought to let him know you're all right."

"Not yet." She sounded hard; she sat bolt upright and tossed her head, resentful, angry with him for having broken the spell.

He said, "Why?"

"It's a long story." She was curt.

"Look, I didn't mean to step on a sore corn. I'm sorry. But he must be climbing the walls by now."

"Good—let him."

"You really hate his guts, don't you?"

"Yes. No—oh hell, Mitch, I don't know." She pulled the towel up over her like a bedsheet and lay back. "Do you really want to hear about me, the sad story of my life?"

"Do you want to tell it?"

"Why not?" she said; and she did.

"My mother is still in the home," she concluded. "He drove her into that. He drove my brother to suicide. He's never had *time* for any of us, Mitch, and that's why. That's why I want him to endure the silence, wondering. My silence will hurt him the way his hurt us all. I want him to have plenty of time to think about that."

He said, "Maybe it's none of my business, but it seems to me it won't get your mother out of the sanitarium and it won't bring your brother back to life and it won't make you any happier. And I imagine your old man's too old to be changed by anything you do at this late date—you may hurt him but you won't change him."

"What am I supposed to do, then—forgive him?"

"I don't suppose you ever could. But maybe you're hurting yourself more than you're hurting him. That kind of hate sort of festers inside you—it can eat you away like some kind of acid, you know? It's not going to do you any good."

"You sound like a schoolteacher," she said sarcastically. " 'This will hurt me worse than it hurts you.' "

"Couldn't you just make some kind of truce with him and go your own separate way?"

"I mean to. But first I—look, I don't want to talk about it any more, all right?"

"If you say so. Only—well, a little while ago you and I made love and I kind of got the feeling it meant something to both of us. Didn't it?"

Her answer was a long time coming. "Yes. It did, Mitch."

"Then if you're going to fill yourself full of hate, how much room's left in you for——?" He left it unfinished, unsaid; he rolled his head to the side and looked straight at her.

Watching him, her eyes slowly filled with tears. She groped

for his hand but he pulled away and got off the bed. His face hardened and he said, "I told you I was stupid. This is all ridiculous. I'm the guy that kidnaped you, remember? Shit, we'd make a great couple—a rich beautiful Ivy League debutante and a crummy flat-busted guitar player with a twenty-to-life rap hanging over my head. Sure—sure."

"It doesn't have to be like that, Mitch. I wouldn't press any charges against you, you know that."

"You wouldn't have to. Your old man will be glad to take care of that little item."

She didn't have any ready answer for that. He turned away, feeling blue and bleak, and went into the bathroom. His drawers and socks were still wet but he put them on. The shirt was damp but he put that on too, and came out of the bathroom ramming his shirttails into his trousers. "Listen, it's a funny thing but every week or so I do get hungry. Suppose we go get something to eat. I hope you like Mexican food."

"I love it," she said. She appeared to have joined in an unspoken agreement not to reopen the previous discussion. When she got to her feet she held the towel against her, picked up her clothes and went into the bathroom, and by shutting the door against him seemed to be shutting him out of her intimate life just as surely as she had opened it to him a short while before. And so when she reappeared in her dress he made his face a blank mask and said, "Okay, we're just two people who happened to meet one night in the desert. We'll leave it like that."

She surprised him: she said, "I won't leave it like that even if you will. Mitch, I thought I came on this crazy thing because I wanted revenge on my father, and it's true, I did—I still do. But that wasn't all. A little while ago I came out of the shower and saw you lying there and I knew I'd really come with you because I just wanted to be with you. If I'd let you leave me along the road somewhere I'd never have seen you again, and I didn't want to lose you. Maybe it's just a delirious reaction to this whole weird thing we've been through—maybe it's something I'll get over when I wake up one morning and the nightmare's over. But I want to have a chance to find out. If that's the way it turns out I won't be scared to say so—let's keep it clean and honest between us, can we?"

"We can try," he said, and began to turn toward the door. Suddenly he went rigid. "My God. What time is it?" He looked at his watch and his face fell. "Jesus, you know how long we've been here? It's almost eight o'clock. That damned *farmacia's* bound to be closed by now—they pull in the sidewalks at sunset in these towns, don't they?"

"We'll find him in the morning, then," she said, practical and unruffled. She had remarkable resilience—perhaps all women did, but he wasn't experienced enough to tell. She said, "Anyhow we're in no condition to face up to Floyd tonight. We need a good solid meal and a long night's sleep, and time to think out what we're going to do. My brain's too fuzzy for that right now and I imagine yours is too."

"I guess," he said, and put his head down, thinking. "Matter of fact, I *have* got one or two ideas, but I don't want you to get caught in the middle. You've been through enough."

"If you're leading up to a suggestion that I ought to go home, forget it, Mitch."

"Look, Floyd's on the run from big trouble. Now what do you think he'd do to anybody who got in his way?"

"I know. But even a train stops, Mitch—something's bound to fracture that superman complex of his. We can do it."

"I'm glad you're so sure of that."

"We can do it," she said again, firmly, and followed him to the door; but then she said in a different voice, "Why's he like that, anyway?"

"Floyd? He was born a son of a bitch. He doesn't need reasons." He held the door for her and then walked over to the adjacent room and knocked. There was no reply; the lights were on and through the window he could see the room was empty, the bed undisturbed, the bathroom door wide open and the bathroom light switched off.

"She's not here," he said, suddenly cold. His glance whipped around the swimming pool but it was deserted.

Terry said, "She probably only went somewhere to eat."

"And not tell us first? What if she went to Floyd?" He was shaking; he grinned loosely. "Look at me. Nerves of steel. Tower of strength. Maybe we both ought to get the hell out of here."

Terry said, "The car's still here. She hasn't gone far. Let's not jump to conclusions, Mitch—Billie Jean isn't a threat to us. She's in just as much trouble as you and Floyd are. She won't go running to the police."

"I wasn't worried about that. But what if she decided to join up with Floyd? If she tells him we're looking for him, he'll be waiting for us. He'd just as soon kill us as step on an ant—and down here there wouldn't even be any questions asked. They kill you around here for your shoes and wristwatch. It happens all the time. A couple of gringo tourists found dead in some alley —who'd bother?"

Terry said, "Let's go have dinner and sleep on it. We'll think better in the morning."

"I don't know," he said, but he went with her.

CHAPTER **Sixteen**

It wasn't all that long after dark but Caborca at night was like Barstow at three o'clock in the morning. That was the morose judgment of Charley Bass as he moved machine-like through the streets, his heavy shoes thudding, empty-eyed in a wilted shirt. Charley Bass was a jaded Yankee slicker with a tired masculine appearance, thin hair combed carefully over the pink scalp, square chin tucked close to his chest on the short wide neck and powerful shoulders of a thick frame that had played collegiate football fifteen years ago and hadn't yet begun to fatten up too badly.

A bum staggered near with his palm outstretched. Charley Bass gave him a synthetic capped-teeth smile and pressed a coin into his palm and the bum breathed profuse thanks over him in a wash of beer-breath. All along the street there were girls leaning against the walls in dark doorways and Charley Bass gave them each his practiced appraisal before he moved on. Most of them, when you got up close, were fat and filthy; one was a boozy raddled old whore who poked her anxious face forward above her ropy neck and spat on the ground when Charley Bass went by shaking his head no. He felt hard-up horny but not so hard-up he wanted to risk a dose of crabs or native *siflis*.

He turned a corner and saw the sputtering fizzy neon of beer signs around the plaza a block away; he went that way, past a weathered fence. Tomcats yelled passionately somewhere in the darkness nearby and one cat streaked slyly across the dark top of the fence, stopped midway and stood arched on its claws. Charley Bass picked up a stone and hurled it at the cat. There was a yowl and the cat disappeared. He went on, tasting the sour flavor of bile, remembering in an unhappy rush of images the golden-thighed Hollywood girls with no last names, the series of middle-aged nymphomaniacs, last month's sticky affair with that banal woman in Barstow. Somehow he never seemed to attract the kind of woman he wanted to attract.

A cacophony of trumpet-guitar music assaulted him on the square, coming out of the open-walled fronts of three cantinas which stood open to the plaza like penny arcades. He stopped outside the first one, a dank place that smelled of urine and beer, and swept it with a quick scrutiny, and went on along the sidewalk. He was about to pass by the second cantina, which seemed even dingier than the first, but he saw a girl eating a taco at a back table and he stopped, went back, and twisted in through the crowded doorway.

It was a cheap saloon with pungent atmosphere—two pinball machines, a dark scratched bar like a Western movie saloon set, no bar stools; half a dozen small tables standing on uneven legs on sawdust and grease. There was a straightforward row of bottles—cheap wine, Mexican beer, rum and tequila—under a wall crowded with beer posters, dusty snapshots, and half a dozen broken rusty old guns of the sort obtainable at a hock shop for ten or fifteen pesos. The terrible band stood around at the far end of the bar, four musicians, one tooting a raucous trumpet and the others playing guitars of various sizes and resonances. There was a great deal of smoke and noise. Charley Bass tried to remember whether it was Thursday or Friday night. There were plenty of people in the place. Almost all of them looked like locals; Caborca wasn't a tourist town.

Except the girl. She was from the States, that was obvious. Charley Bass crowded up to the bar and after an exercise in bad Spanish and sign language managed to buy a glass of black beer which he sipped as he turned his back to the bar and studied the girl over the rim of his glass.

Her dress was soiled, her fingernails dirty, her hair tangled in ropy disorder, but she was big and sloppy and exciting, her mouth full and sensuous, her eyes pushing out a sleepy, provocative sexual aura as tangible as the smell of the bar room. Her hefty hips and big freewheeling breasts made straining curves against her tight soiled dress.

She had a lot of fingerprints on her. But she was a girl who wanted sensation and did as she pleased: a woman in heat.

Charley Bass bought another beer and carried it over to her table. "May I join you? I'm unarmed."

She looked up; her cranky, pouty expression changed. Charley Bass adjusted his smile, ready for her rebuff. The girl picked up her margarita and drank fast; some of it ran down her chin. He realized, what he hadn't seen before, that she had had quite a few. Her eyes were slightly vague and she almost upset the glass when she set it down. She stared moodily at him and stuck out a pudgy index finger to swirl the ice cube in the squat glass; she still hadn't said a word. The air around her was thick with the heavy scent of cheap perfume.

Finally she spoke but her voice was pitched low and he couldn't make out what she said against the heavy background of talk and laughter. He bent down, staring at the heavy lard-white mass of bunched cleavage visible in the scoop-neck of her dress. "Beg pardon?"

"I said siddown."

"Thanks." He settled into a fragile-looking chair across from her. When he put his elbow on the table it rocked toward him. It was a tiny table, hardly large enough for two drinks and four elbows. Noise and crowd swirled close-packed around them. He said, "I'm Charley Bass."

"Good for you."

He put on his hearty red-cheeked smile. "Hell of a town to get stuck in, isn't it?"

"You can say that again."

He wondered how old she was. Twenty-five, maybe; getting a little too soft and suety. A few years more and she'd start getting passed down the line until some smart guy came along and took her on a little vacation to Hong Kong or South America, and then they'd cop her passport and unload her into a crib where she'd get beat all the way down until she didn't even *want* to go home. He knew: he'd plied that trade himself.

She was watching him sleepily. He said, "Here I had a great weekend all set up, meet some friends down at Rocky Point and go out on their boat for marlin in the Gulf. But what happens? My damn Buick blows a wheel-bearing five miles up the road and I spend the whole damn day getting a tow back to this lousy town. Stuck here till morning now. How do you like that?"

"Yeah," she said. "We had a breakdown too, back up the road. Seven stinking hours in this heat before the good-for-nothin' grease monkey got the water pump fixed."

He said quickly, "We?"

"Yeah, some—some people I hitched a ride with." Her restless eyes shifted away, combing the crowd.

His hands felt sticky. "You don't mean to tell me you're alone here? What a godawful place."

"You can say that again."

"How about another drink, hey?"

"You paying?"

"Of course, honey."

"Okay, then. I'm kind of short, you know? The guy with the bugle over there bought me these, but then some fat Mexican woman came in and dragged him away by the ear." She didn't laugh. "His wife, I guess. Seven or eight months pregnant from what I could see. Poor son of a bitch must be pretty uptight if she keeps after him like that all the time. Why didn't she just let him enjoy himself? Who'd be hurt by it?"

"It wouldn't have bothered you?"

"Me? I like it, they like it. What's wrong with that?"

"Well," Charley Bass said, "you know these Catholics."

"I was raised Catholic. I know all about it."

"Say, what'd you say your name was?"

"Billie Jean. I forgot your name."

"Charley Bass. Like Sam Bass, the Texas outlaw, ever heard of him?"

"I don't know. You related to him or something?"

"Who knows?" He turned and signaled the barmaid. She

came over with a cork-lined metal tray and a bored face and Charley Bass made a circular gesture to order another round; the barmaid turned away, expressionless, giving no indication whether she had understood the order.

He shifted his chair forward when he turned back to face the table. His knee touched against Billie Jean's and she did not withdraw; he gave her a lidded smile and said, "I'm in the oil business. Buy and sell leases. From Pasadena, believe it or not. How about you?"

"Oh, I'm from—just around, you know."

His hand, under the table, explored her thigh. Under the thin fabric of her dress he saw her nipples grow, harden and swell. Her eyelids drooped and she squirmed on the chair. He said, "I got a room in the old hotel a couple of blocks up the street. How about it, Billie Jean? Nice way to pass the time."

"Maybe," she said. A crafty light came into her eyes. "Look, Mister Charley Bass, maybe you'd like to do a girl a favor."

"Just name it."

"Well, it's like this, see—these people I, uh, hitched a ride with, they're still here in town, but when I came along with them I didn't know what they were like. I found out they're, you know, *involved* in something kind of shady-like. I ain't sure what it is," she added hastily, "maybe dope smuggling or something, but I'm pretty sure they think I'm onto them on account of something one of them let slip in the car. Soon as we got here I split, you know? They ain't come looking for me but just the same I'd just as soon not see them again, you know what I mean? They're pretty tough, you know?"

He reached out and patted her hand. "I'll be glad to give you a ride, honey."

"Well, it——"

She broke off because the barmaid had returned. The barmaid set down drinks on the table and waited indifferently until Charley Bass paid her, whereupon she counted the money laboriously and turned away without a word or a nod.

Billie Jean said, "It ain't just a ride I need."

"What, then?"

"Well, these people I was with, they've still got my papers.

You know, my tourist permit. Mister, I don't want to go back there and face them just to get that piece of paper. I tell them I want my permit back and they'll sure as hell think there's something fishy going on, you know? Maybe think I'm gonna turn them over to the cops or something. They're a pretty mean bunch, you know?"

Charley Bass said, "Well, I don't know, honey. It's pretty tough getting back through the border without papers."

"I thought maybe you'd know a way."

"I might," he said, and pretended to think on it. Billie Jean leaned toward him with a moist hot smile; the dress slipped off her shoulder and one huge breast almost slipped its moorings— a deliberate movement and one which she undoubtedly had practiced to an art. He thought about it. She had a vapid conventional mind, desolate and predictable; she wouldn't be any trouble. A few nights of hot sex with her and then maybe he could look up Sweeney in Hermosillo—Sweeney was in the skin trade, or had been, and a lush-bodied girl stranded in Mexico without papers was just Sweeney's meat. Sweeney would give Charley Bass a cut of the profits. If Sweeney was still there. It had been some time since Charley Bass had conned his way up out of that league but he was a little strapped right now and a few hundred extra wouldn't hurt any. *Why not?*

Billie Jean said throatily, "Be a buddy, mister. You know what'll happen if I get caught without that damned permit. I get a couple years of laundry-hands and starchy prison food to spread out on and ain't nobody ever gonna look twice at me again. Listen, they put you in jail down here, you know what happens to you. The American consul never heard of you. Piss and dirt in some old cell they used to use back when they fought Indians. Big stinky Indian butches crawling all over you and you rot on pinto-bean dysentery. They won't even let a white woman work, like a Mexican citizen prisoner, make a few pesos on the side."

"You seem to know a lot about it."

"I heard once from a girl I knew. It sent shivers crawlin' up my back just *hearing* about it."

"Sounds pretty grim."

†† 168

"You can say that again. So how about it, lover?"

He covered her hand with his palm and gave it a warm avuncular squeeze. "You just leave it to me, honey. Everything's going to be just fine and dandy."

Billie Jean's plump face lit up. She leaned forward and pulled his head toward her and kissed him with moist warmth and suction

CHAPTER **Seventeen**

The big Cadillac drummed eastward away from the seacoast, its quadruple headlights stabbing the darkness. Twisting through the coastal hills, Carl Oakley had both hands on the wheel at the ten-minutes-to-two position; his head was thrust forward slightly, tense, the eyes concentrated on the pitted road ahead as it sped into the light.

Diego Orozco said, "You want me to drive a while? You're pretty tired."

"I'm all right. I'm fine." He felt alert but jumpy; he had taken two Dexedrines. "Where did we miss them, Diego?"

"Beats shit out of me."

"Your boys seemed too positive they couldn't have got through Rocky Point."

"If they had we'd have picked up a smell of them. They didn't take no boat out, there weren't any airplanes and copters in or out, and the road south along the coast is blocked off for construction. How many times you want to go over all this, Carl? It adds up the same every time."

Oakley stuck a cigar in his mouth and punched the dashboard lighter. "You keep trying to use your head. You figure the thing to do is rule out all the impossibilities and look at whatever you've got left. But what happens when you rule out all the impossibilities and there isn't anything left?"

"Then," said Orozco, "you've overlooked something."

"All right. What?"

"Lots of things, Carl. They didn't do what we expected them to do, that's all. Plenty other things they could've done just as easy. For instance maybe they're holed up making arrangements to get phony papers. False passport, forged seaman's card and papers, you can get a berth on some Liberian freighter bound for Macao and nobody'll ever find you again. All it takes is a little time and the right contacts. Or maybe they figured to draw us off down here on a cold trail and then disappear, filter back into Nogales over the weekend and get back into the States by joining the mob of tourists returning Sunday night from the bullfights."

The lighter had snapped; Oakley pressed it to his cigar and heard it sizzle. He sucked the powerful smoke deep into his lungs and coughed. "But you're sure the bleeper's still working. The batteries haven't had time to die out?"

"I ain't sure of nothing—but theoretically the thing's still alive and well and livin' in that suitcase. We got to get within twenty-five or thirty miles of it before we can pick it up, though."

"It doesn't add up. If they didn't get as far as Rocky Point they've got to be somewhere along this road. Why didn't we pick up the signal if we passed right by them?"

"Maybe they're holed up in a lead mine. Maybe they were too close to a short-wave broadcast station that jammed the signal. Maybe there was a mountain between us and an ionized cloud layer above it. Maybe they discovered the bug and smashed it. Maybe they emptied the suitcase and buried it in a slag heap full of metal ore. Maybe the bleeper was faulty in the first place and ain't working at all. You want ironclad guarantees, Carl? You won't get them from me."

"Maybe if my mother had a beard she'd be my father. I've had maybes up to here."

Orozco sat back, adjusting his bulk, tugging at his amply fleshed throat. He subsided into tight-lipped reserve; when Oakley glanced at him his eyes, reflecting the dim dashboard glow, had an ominous murky color.

The lights of a car rushed forward and passed them; Oakley

glimpsed a family of adults and kids in the long chrome-glinting station wagon, towing a boat on a trailer.

Orozco sat motionless, the smoke of Oakley's cigar making a vague cloud between them. Oakley felt rumpled and haggard. He glanced at the gun glinting dully in Orozco's waistband and said, "Could you kill a man?"

"I have."

"You have? Where?"

"Where you get a medal for it. Korea."

"Not the same thing as I meant. What if we do catch up and they want to make a fight of it?"

Orozco's head turned slowly. "*I'm* not worried about me, Carl."

"All right—all right." Orozco was right, Oakley thought irritably. It was himself he was worried about. Orozco, giving him a gun yesterday, had asked, "How good are you with one of these things?" and he had had to answer, "Not very." It wasn't a question of marksmanship; it was a question of character. He had never been under fire, never aimed a gun at another human being.

The sky ahead was graying up. They covered the next forty miles without talking while dawn came indigo and violet and red and pink and orange. Oakley lowered the visor against the horizon-balanced sun. He felt the glazed, slightly out-of-contact unreality of sleeplessness. His eyes began to stray out of focus and he had to blink frequently and harshly; the eye-sockets felt dry and raw from cigar smoke. There thrummed in his ears a steady soporific beating of engine, tires, wind. The road followed the gentle undulations of arid swells across the uneven desert, mountains heaving their dry-sided bulk against the sky at random intervals in various directions; the road swung along parallel to a dry riverbed, keeping to the low ground. A roadsign loomed and flashed by: *Caborca 20 km.* Shortly thereafter, something began to tweet and twitter in his ears—at first he thought it was an atmospheric change that had set up a ringing; then the sound became so tangible he began to look around the interior of the car to see if a small bird had flown in through the window by mistake.

Orozco said very gently, "Slow it down, Carl." He was bent forward over the portable radio receiver that bulked on the floor between his legs. Half-blinded by sun glare, Oakley could barely make out the rhythmic flash of a dull red lamp on top of the set. Orozco was turning dials in his big fists; the beeping sound grew louder and softer as he adjusted the coordinates. He brought it back up to its loudest pitch and made a mark on the map in his lap. "Somewhere south of us," he muttered. "Southeast. Keep going a couple miles and we'll take another fix, try and triangulate him down."

Oakley's solemn features had slowly lost their weariness; "By God. We've got the sons of bitches."

"Maybe. Maybe all's we got is an empty suitcase. We'll see."

"No," Oakley said. "No. It's them. It's got to be. We've got 'em, Diego!"

Orozco only murmured, "Maybe ten miles away off to the right there. Let's see if we can find a road goes in that direction." He bent his head over the map and moved a stubby finger along it.

Mitch parked the Ford in front of the *farmacia* and sat for a moment brooding at the place, elbows curled over the steering wheel. Terry Conniston said, "Do you want me to go in with you?"

"No. Floyd won't be too suprised if I show up alone. He will be, if you're with me."

"What makes you think he's in there?"

"I don't. I just can't think of anyplace else to look. Maybe he's not here at all. Maybe Billie Jean blew the whistle and they both took off somewhere. Oh, Christ, I'm just stalling. You keep your head down, okay?"

He turned his solemn glance on her and leaned back, reaching around with his right hand to lift the door handle under his left elbow. Terry put out a hand to stop him; she slid closer along the seat and presented her face and he kissed her before he got out. Her eyes held him through the windshield when he walked around the front of the car and climbed the steps. He put his back to her and set his jaw, hooked his hand over the revolver butt in his hip pocket and swung the door open to beard von Roon's den.

The woman behind the counter was the only person in the place that he could see. There was a laboratory behind the sales room, part of which he could see through an open door; there was another door at the back, closed, leading perhaps to a flight of stairs to the floor overhead.

The woman fixed her glance on Mitch as if she was waiting for him to serve a subpoena on her. She had a sagging jaundiced face, easy to take for an Oriental's; by her cheekbones and black ropy hair she was evidently a *mestizo*. Mitch strolled to the counter, measuring the thud of his pulse against the casualness of his bearing; he said in his rusty guidebook Spanish, *"Yo deseo a conocer al señor von Roon."* He added as an afterthought, *"Por favor."*

"El doctor no está aquí."

"Uh—dónde está, por favor?" He knew all his grammar was wrong but she obviously understood what he was trying to say. He clutched the gun, out of her sight, and looked around nervously.

The Indian woman gave him a cool, contemptuous appraisal; she said, *"Quíen sabe?"* and began to move away.

With his left hand Mitch crumpled a five-dollar bill in his pocket and took it out. The woman paused, looking at him. He rolled the bill into a greenish wad, tight as a spitball, and let it roll casually across the counter toward her. *"Es muy importante."* She probably thought he was a dope addict or a boy friend looking for an abortionist but he didn't care what she thought.

She picked up the wad and smoothed it out. Her expression did not change. She said, *"Está en la Ciudad México. Volveré martés."* He was in Mexico City: he would return Tuesday. She gave him an arch smile and pocketed the five dollars.

Shaking, he took another bill out of his pocket and looked at it. Ten dollars. Deliberately, he ripped it in half and pushed one half across the counter. *"Por favor, dígame. Hay un joven Yanqui, muy duro, con pelo negro, tal guapo—con ojos muy—uh, malignos. Comprende? Estaba aquí?"* It was a limp description of Floyd—young Yankee, very hard, black hair, perhaps handsome, with very evil eyes—and he hadn't held out much hope of getting anywhere with it: but he saw the woman's face change and he knew he had scored a hit. The pulse thudded harder in him; he made a vague gesture with the half of the ten-dollar bill. *"Dígame—dónde está este Yanqui?"*

She spoke slowly, frowning, saying yes, there had been such a one; he had come seeking the Doctor von Roon and he had been told the same thing, that *el Doctor* would not return from Mexico City until Tuesday, perhaps even later. She kept her eyes on the half-bill in Mitch's fist and Mitch shook his head and pressed her: *"Dónde está ahora?"* Where is he *now?*

"El Doctor?"

"No. El Yanqui." He waved the torn money at her, leaning forward, his face fierce and furious.

She began to speak and he had to stop her and tell her to start over again and go slower. She did; she said with unconcealed impatience with his linguistic limitations that the Yanqui had left word where *el Doctor* could reach him but that she was to tell no one this except *el Doctor.* But when she said this her gaze was fixed on the torn bill in Mitch's fist. Mitch reached into his pocket for the third time and withdrew the last money he had —another fiver—and added it to the torn half of the ten in his fist. *"Es todo. No hay más."* He turned out his pocket to show her.

She considered the money and she considered his face. She said, *"Usted—está un amigo del Yanqui?"*

Not exactly a friend of his, Mitch thought; but he didn't know how to phrase it in Spanish and so he merely shook his head at her. She was watching him in a way that made him morally certain she had disliked Floyd violently: Floyd had probably frightened her. And so, taking a chance, Mitch took the revolver out of his hip pocket and showed it to her, and put it away again, implying—he hoped—that it wasn't friendship that made him seek the *Yanqui.*

She took a while to make up her mind; finally she rattled off something decisive; he had to make her repeat it twice, at the end of which time she was exasperated with him and he was grimly satisfied. He left all the money on the counter and walked out of the place into the blaze of sunshine and said to Terry in the car window, "He's hiding out in a shack south of here—up in those hills." He went around and got in. She didn't say anything; she only watched him. He took the gun out and snapped it open and stared at the six brassy new cartridge cases with their silver-colored primers. He had a pocketful more. He snapped it shut and put it on his lap and started the car.

They had to crawl the Ford through morning knots of pedestrians in the narrow curving streets. The early daylight streamed through the tall palm trees, its color very rich. They went past the old mission church at the edge of town and he saw distinctly the pocked bullet holes in its adobe façade. Small dogs ran yapping after the car until it cleared the last palms at the southern limit of Caborca. Mitch told Terry what had happened inside the pharmacy; he said, "Floyd probably threatened to kill her if she told anybody but twenty dollars was more money than she'd ever seen in her life. She saw my gun and she probably figures I'll kill Floyd for her—I wish I was as sure of myself as she seemed to be. Down here they think a man's got a hell of a lot of *machismo* and *cojones* if he sports a gun."

"That was Floyd's gun, wasn't it? He hasn't got another one."

"Knowing Floyd, he's got an arsenal out here with him if he thinks he needs one. Guns are easy enough to come by down here if you've got the money to pay for them. Everything's for sale down here. Jesus, Terry, I'm just talking to keep from going through the roof—maybe we better forget this whole thing and turn around."

"Is that what you want to do?"

He had been thinking about very little else; but now he thought about it yet again and he realized with startling sudden clarity that these past days had secretly created resolve inside him. All his life he had failed at things. He didn't know whether it was hysteria or courage but whatever it was, even if he failed again this time it would not be for want of trying. It occurred to him, in a way he sensed but could not explain even to himself, that he might lose more by turning away from this than he stood to lose even if he failed against Floyd.

And so he took himself a little by surprise when he answered her question: "No. I guess I have to prove something."

"You don't need to prove anything to anybody, Mitch."

"I need to prove something to myself. Does that make any sense?"

"I guess it does, after all."

The dirt road crabbed its way up into the beige-colored hills, full of rocks with square corners and washed-out ruts; the Ford strained and lurched at slow speed. "She said it was the far side of the hill from the big rock that looks like a hat. Must have meant that one up there. I think I'll leave the car there and leave you in it. Be better to go down on foot—maybe I can catch him by surprise."

"I don't want to wait in the car, Mitch."

"I'll have trouble enough watching him without looking out for you too. What the hell is that?"

It was a car—a dusty Cadillac gleaming in the sun, parked in the road by the hat-shaped boulder. It might have been imagination but he thought he could still smell the dust in the air from its passage: it must have arrived just before them. Scowling, he halted the Ford behind the Cadillac's bumper and got out, closing his hand around the gun, and walked quickly toward the crest of the hill. He heard Terry get out of the car behind him and he glanced over his shoulder to wave her back, but she kept coming and he didn't want to lift his voice; he only gestured again and went on, getting up on his toes and beginning to run with a sense of instinctive urgency. It was then that he heard the gunshot.

CHAPTER **Eighteen**

Oakley thought with bitter anguish, *He set it up beautifully and we walked right into it.*

The tumbledown shack stood in the full glare of the sun fifty yards downhill from them in a nest of splintered boulders; the Oldsmobile stood alongside the shack and cooking smoke rose from the chimney. Standing bolt still, Oakley slowly turned his head to look back past Orozco's frozen bulk toward the rocks high to their left from which the gunshot had come. The bullet had screamed off the dirt not three feet in front of Oakley's boot toe; it had brought them both up short and now a voice issued from the rocks—a cool deep voice Oakley recognized at once from telephone calls:

"Just stand still where you are and turn around so I can see you—slowly if you please; haste might make me nervous."

Orozco's bootsoles crunched the earth as he made a slow ponderous wheel, keeping his arms well away from his body. Oakley stood fast, head cocked over his shoulder. He saw Floyd Rymer come out of the rocks moving like a big cat, all liquid grace and feline power, balancing a large automatic pistol on them. There was no mistaking Rymer's identity—the glossy photographs had captured his likeness perfectly. All except the eyes: hard, penetrating, yet utterly devoid of emotion.

"All right," said Floyd Rymer. "The car belongs to Conniston but who are you?"

Oakley made no answer; his narrowed glance steadied on Rymer's gun and he felt sweat pour down his face. He heard Orozco say, "Let's say we work for Mr. Conniston."

"Fine. Thumb and forefinger, now, both of you lift those pistols out of your belts and toss them on the ground. Don't try any cowboy tricks because we all know I've got nothing to lose by killing you. They'd probably never find your bodies."

Oakley glanced at Orozco but Orozco made no signal; he only obeyed instructions by slowly lifting the revolver from his waistband and letting it drop on the ground a yard away from his boots. Oakley began to tremble; he did not stir until Orozco growled, "Do what he wants, Carl."

When he picked the gun out of his belt he lost his grip on it and it fell down the front of his trousers, banged off his knee and skittered away in the dirt. A twitch lifted one corner of Floyd Rymer's mouth.

Floyd said, "How'd you trace me here?"

Orozco said promptly, "They picked up your license number when you crossed the border at Lochiel."

Floyd rested his shoulder against a tall rock. "No good—try again. I've switched plates twice since I crossed over."

Oakley's nostrils dilated; he felt faint in the burning sun. Orozco said, "All right. There's a radio bug in the ransom suitcase."

Floyd Rymer's eyebrows lifted half an inch. "I salute you," he said. "Thanks for warning me—I'll have to attend to that. Who else is around here? How many others behind you—and how far?"

Oakley said, "Don't tell him, Diego."

"I wasn't plannin' to," Orozco drawled. "Look, Rymer, we know your names, we found the two dead ones you left in Soledad. You can't get away even if you do shoot both of us. The whole world knows who you are. Now you turn over the money to us and tell us where we can find Terry Conniston and maybe we'll think about letting you cop a plea."

Floyd Rymer smiled very slowly. It was the most terrifying expression Oakley had ever witnessed on a human face. Oakley's breathing was tight and shallow; his sphincter contracted, his palms dripped. Floyd lifted the automatic and Oakley clearly saw the knuckles begin to whiten; he knew that Rymer was going to shoot them both in their tracks.

A voice rammed down from the splintered boulders above: "Stop it, Floyd!"

Oakley saw the rest in a blur, as if it were a dream: forever afterward he tried to bring it back but it never came clear to him, there was only a wheeling kaleidoscope of impressions. Floyd's head whipped around; Orozco began to move; there was a woman's scream, thin in the high air; a youth standing above Floyd Rymer with a police revolver cocked; the frenzied glitter of Floyd Rymer's eyes as the impassive expression suddenly broke and the handsome leonine face became a twisted ugly mask of fury. There was shooting: Floyd Rymer and the youth exchanging shots, both of them ducking and wheeling. The brass sun spinning overhead. Orozco ducking to the ground, scooping up his gun, coming up on one knee with amazing agility. One image stood out clear: the sudden jump and puff of a bullet striking the youth in the hip by his trouser pocket, the youth knocked down asprawl in the boulders by the impact of the big slug. The youth had fired a fussilade of shots but none of them had hit Floyd Rymer; Floyd came around and Oakley was staring down the muzzle of the automatic and he heard the great ear-splitting roar of two or three or four gunshots, a deafening rattle like artillery in his ear. Afterward he realized it had been Orozco, coolly and methodically pumping bullets into Floyd Rymer like a sharpshooter on a rifle range. Oakley had no recollection of Floyd falling, no recollection of the next few seconds; somewhere in the ensuing run of time he realized he had picked up his gun and walked forward, for he found himself standing above Floyd Rymer's dead body with the unfired pistol clutched in his fist. Orozco was kneeling down by the corpse and two people were coming down out of the rocks together, the youth hobbling on one leg and leaning his weight on Terry Conniston.

Oakley turned a comatose stare on them. "Terry." His voice was a disembodied croak, not his own. Weakness flowed along his fibers: his body went flaccid and he sat down clumsily, abruptly. A red haze filmed his eyes and he almost lost consciousness; he drifted in a mist.

Rymer's body must have cleared all its functions at the moment of death. The air stank of excrement. It was that olfactory foulness that brought him out of it, as if it were spirits of ammonia. When he stood up the muscles of his legs hardly supported him.

He met Orozco's glance. Orozco's sunken eyes had gone charcoal black: his round face was bitter. Oakley turned clumsily to face Terry Conniston—his eyes observed without believing. There was a disturbing tremor behind his knees.

Terry said to him, "What the devil are you doing here?"

The four of them congregated on the front step of the shack; Oakley thought vaguely that Floyd Rymer must have had a predilection for abandoned habitations—first Soledad ghost town, now this deserted 'dobe. Mitch Baird sat against the wall with his legs stretched out, Terry ministering his wound—not much of a wound; Floyd's bullet had dug a shallow trench along the side of his hip. Oakley found the strength to say, "That's a funny way to treat a man that kidnaped you."

Terry said without looking up, "He saved your life, didn't he? Doesn't that count for anything with you?"

"I don't get any of this," Oakley said helplessly.

"Nobody asked you to."

Orozco was opening the trunk compartment of the Oldsmobile. Oakley watched him lean over and heard the snap of suitcase locks and saw Orozco lift the lid of the suitcase into view. Orozco said, "I think it's all here."

Terry said, "You can give it back to my father. I'm sure he'll be thrilled."

Oakley's eyes widened. "Your father is——" He couldn't finish it.

"A first-class son of a bitch," Terry said. "We heard about what he said on the phone. As if he cared more about getting revenge than saving my life."

"That wasn't your father on the phone," Oakley said. "Where the hell have you been?"

Mitch Baird said, "She's been with me."

"You. That's fine. That's just dandy. Kid, do you happen to know what kind of trouble you're in?"

Terry looked up, drawn and furious. "You're just like him, aren't you, Carl? You never let simple things like gratitude stand in your way, do you? *Mitch saved your life!*"

"I know he did. But it doesn't change the fact that——"

Terry bounced to her feet. "Shut up, Carl. Just shut up, will you? You just take that damned money back to my father and get a receipt for it and tell him I don't ever want to see him again. Tell him Mitch and I are going away together. He ought to get a boost out of that."

Grim as a pallbearer, Oakley planted his feet and dragged a hand across his eyes and said, "I can't tell your father anything, Terry. He's dead. He's been dead since the night you were kidnaped."

Terry's reactions baffled him; but then everything baffled him. Oakley felt as if he had lost his grip on reality; he sensed he was going mad.

She had gone from shock to rage; she had stormed, spiteful and willful; she had gone off into the rocks and he had heard the sound of her retching and seen the signs of misery on Mitch Baird's wan face. But then she had come back, subdued, and she had sat down beside Mitch and groped for Mitch's hand and Oakley stood above the two of them watching them and simply did not understand any of it.

And then Terry said, "I can't tell you how sorry I am, Carl."

"Are *you* apologizing to *me?* What for?"

"For hating him," she said. "Maybe that doesn't make sense to you. He's dead? I still can't get it into my head, Carl. There were things we had to say to each other—it isn't fair."

Oakley saw Mitch grip her hand in both of his; Mitch murmured, "Take it easy."

Something burst inside Oakley: he roared, "What in the God damned hell is *his* part in this?"

Both of them looked up at him, and after a while they told him.

Oakley had to absorb it. He turned a dumbfounded face toward Orozco, and the fat man said in his quiet way, "You can't prosecute him anyway, Carl, in case you forgot. There never was any kidnaping—remember?" Orozco came away from the car and said, "Walk off a little piece here with me, Carl," and Oakley, too wilted to question him, followed obediently.

Orozco took him around the corner into the shade and said, "We got a few things to talk through, Carl. Right now." An odd light burned in his eyes. When Oakley made no sign of resistance the fat man said, "You're going to have to tell them the whole thing, you know. It's the only way you can convince them not to talk about this, ever. You got to make a deal with them —promise you won't expose the Baird kid. In return they promise not to expose you. Nobody ever mentions that there was a kidnaping. You get to keep Conniston's business, or most of it anyway, and Louise gets her inheritance, and these two kids get to keep each other. And just maybe it might be a good idea if you sweetened the pot a little by givin' them a wedding present, like say that half million dollars in cash. How about it, then?"

"Nuts. I don't have to tell them a damned thing."

"Sure you do." Orozco began to smile. "Because if you don't I will."

Oakley rested his back against the grimy wall, tipped his head back and closed his eyes. "You're not finished, are you?"

"Uh-unh. You understand me now, Carl—price is high, my price for not exposin' you. Because once you get done setting up with these two kids you're going to sign the Conniston ranch over to me."

Oakley said, softly, finally, "You made it work, didn't you, Diego?"

"You always used to tell me to grab an opportunity when I saw one."

"I never thought you wanted the ranch."

"Oh, I don't mean to keep it. But once I give it all back to the *chicanos,* the whole damn land grant, I'm gonna have every Spanish vote in the country in my pocket, and a lot of Anglo liberal votes right along with them. And the funny thing is I'm gonna make a pretty damn good politician, Carl. With your help. Have I got it?"

Oakley opened his eyes. He felt strong again, decisive. "Sure you have," he said. He clapped Orozco on the shoulder and said, "You're the meanest bastard I ever met, amigo, and it's a pleasure knowing you." He grinned, and turned to walk around to the front of the shack.

Orozco came after him, smiling.

Oakley came around the corner and saw Terry and Mitch sitting together with their arms around each other's waists. They looked up when he appeared; they looked uncertain, afraid, slightly punch-drunk. Oakley felt full of self-confidence —strong, sure, warm with benevolence. He said, "We've got a lot of things to clear up but everything's going to be all right. Will you both take my word for that?"

They just watched him, not so much suspicious as puzzled. Oakley hunkered down on his heels beside them in the shade of the adobe wall and put an unlit cigar in the corner of his mouth and before he began to talk he looked up past Orozco's looming hulk at the hard brassy sky above the rock hills. A few diaphanous cirrus clouds moved languorously overhead and a buzzard began to circle down toward Floyd Rymer's body.

A B O U T   T H E   A U T H O R

BRIAN GARFIELD was born in New York City but grew up in Tucson, Arizona. As a young writer he made a highly successful debut in the field of Western fiction. He published over forty books and was the youngest president of the Western Writers of America. A man of many talents, Mr. Garfield surprised the entire literary establishment by the unheard-of and successful switch from his earlier writing concerns to a continuing series of novels of suspense and works of nonfiction. Some of his current writing reflects his detailed knowledge of the West, its landscape, history, and people, while each of his books demonstrates his ability to incorporate another element of his colorful experience. In the case of *What of Terry Conniston?* Mr. Garfield drew on his mixed experiences as a leader of a rock group.

He and Mrs. Garfield live on an impressively tax-ridden 150-year-old estate on the Delaware River near Lambertville, New Jersey. His constant poker partners include Donald Westlake, Lawrence Block, and William Tenn.